A Cassandra Mystery™

MYSTERY IN HOLLYWOOD

BY JENNIFER AUSTIN

ILLUSTRATED BY
ANN MEISEL

A BYRON PREISS BOOK

PUBLISHERS • GROSSET & DUNLAP • NEW YORK
A MEMBER OF THE PUTNAM PUBLISHING GROUP

Library of Congress Catalog Card Number: 89-84099

ISBN 0-448-37702-0

A B C D E F G H I J

Special thanks to Robin Stevenson

Cover painting by Ann Meisel
Book design by Alex Jay/Studio J

"*L*et's use the pink gel, Cassie," yelled the stage manager from fourteen feet below. "It'll soften the set."

Straddling the grid high above the stage, Cassie B. Jones held two squares of plastic, one pink and one amber, in her left hand. With her right hand she hung on for dear life.

"Okay," she called back, fitting the pink gel into the black metal frame of the spotlight. "How does it look?"

"That's great!" The stage manager checked his watch. "Hey, I'll see you here one week from to-day." And he was gone.

As Cassie leaned down to step back onto the ladder, her honey-blond hair tumbled around her face, hiding brown eyes that smiled. Cassie was proud of herself. She'd landed the perfect job at the Milltown Mystery Playhouse. As an apprentice, she was learning about her two favorite things—acting and mysteries. Someday she hoped to become a famous actress or a famous detective, or both.

On impulse, she paused halfway down the ladder. Ignoring the fact that her white T-shirt with the Playhouse logo was dusty and dirty, forgetting that her face probably matched her shirt, she pulled her hair to the top of her head and raised her chin.

"Well, Cassandra," she said, using her mock-British accent. "Someday you'll look back on this apprenticeship in Milltown, Ohio, and say, 'I paid my dues. I'm a star and I belong here.' "

"Bravo!" called a loud voice from the back of the theater. "And spoken in the spotlight, where a star should always stand."

Cassie realized she was dead center stage. She felt her face getting hot, and scrambled down the ladder to hide her embarrassment. "I was just rehearsing my lines," she said to the man she recognized as the box-office secretary. "I thought I was alone."

"Your accent is pretty good. You ought to be playing the role of Elena—even if she does get murdered in Act Two."

They both laughed, then Cassie put the amber gel on the table and started up the aisle.

"Oh, Cassie," said the secretary, "someone named Alexandra Bennett is trying to reach you."

"Alex!" exclaimed Cassie. "She phoned here from England?"

"No, your kid sister called you from home. She

was excited. Alexandra—the name sounds like royalty. Who is she?''

Cassie halted her mad dash for the parking lot long enough to explain. ''She's my pen pal and dearest friend. We've been writing for more than three years. I even flew to England to meet her.'' Cassie didn't mention that she'd solved a mystery involving Alex while she was in England. Grabbing her tote bag, Cassie ran to her car.

While Cassie maneuvered through traffic, she thought about all that had happened in so short a time. High school graduation, getting the apprenticeship at the Playhouse for a year, and the surprise invitation and trip to England to attend Alex's debut ball.

On her visit she'd been drawn into a dangerous mystery that gave her the chance to become the detective she'd always dreamed she could be. Since then, she'd had the chance to use her detective skills again when she'd joined Alex at the Kentucky Derby.

If Alex was calling her now instead of writing . . . Wow, could it mean another case? Cassie concentrated on her driving so she wouldn't speed.

When she pulled into the driveway of her house, Grandma Jones was waiting at the front door. ''Hurry, Cassie,'' she called. ''Alexandra's on the phone again.''

Melanie, Cassie's ten-year-old sister, was jumping up and down beside the phone, holding on to her horn-rimmed glasses with one finger. "Hurry, Cassie! Alex is calling from Hollywood!"

"Hollywood?"

"Yes!" Mel's brown eyes were huge. "From some big studio director's office. Maybe they want you to star in a new movie."

Cassie pretended to punch her sister with one hand and grabbed the phone with the other. "Alex, what are you doing in Hollywood?"

"Hello, Cassandra Best!" said Alex.

Cassie had signed her name *Cassandra Best* the very first time she'd written to Alex. Cassandra Best Jones *was* Cassie's full name, so the pen name wasn't too far from the truth. But the little difference meant a lot to Cassie. Cassandra Best sounded like a glamorous, exciting person—the kind of girl Cassie had always wanted to be. The name made her feel that she could do anything—even solve mysteries.

"I'm here on assignment for Daddy's newspaper," Alex went on. Alex was a society journalist. "You know Rod Taggart, the rock star?"

"Rod Taggart?" Cassie repeated, while Mel immediately pretended to faint. Then she tried to listen in on the conversation.

"Mel, please!" Cassie smiled as Mel ran out to the backyard. Rod Taggart was Mel's favorite rock star. She had covered her side of the bedroom that the two girls shared with posters of him. "Go ahead,

4

Alex. I know who Rod Taggart is. Have you met him?''

''Have I, and he's a darling.'' Alex's voice dropped. ''Can you still hear me, Cassandra?''

''Yes, but why are you whispering?''

''Because I don't want anyone to hear. Rod's in some kind of danger—''

''What do you mean, 'danger'?'' Cassie asked with excitement. This *was* a case!

''He's starring in a horror film called *Witches' Brew.* Cassie, all sorts of trouble is brewing here on the set.''

''What kind of trouble, Alex?''

''Well, the studio's calling them accidents, but I'm sure they're not. Rod's in danger and we need your help.'' There was a terrible urgency in Alex's voice.

''Shouldn't you go to the police?'' Cassie made herself say at the risk of missing out on the case.

Maintaining a hushed voice, Alex said, ''The studio—and Rod, too—wants to avoid any bad publicity, which is what might happen if they call the police. I've told Rod about your detective skills, Cassandra Best.''

Hearing her detective ''alias'' again, Cassie's excitement grew. As Cassandra Best, she'd already solved two cases. The name had brought her good luck before, and she couldn't wait to use it again.

''I hope you haven't told too many people I'm a

5

detective, Alex. If everyone knows, I won't be able to help.''

"I haven't told anyone but Rod, Cassandra. I only told him how you solved my kidnapping single-handedly.''

"Along with Scotland Yard, are you forgetting?''

Alex laughed. "Cassandra, I've arranged to have a prepaid ticket to Los Angeles waiting for you at the airport. Don't even bother to pack—I've brought more than enough clothes for both of us.''

"I'll have to ask Gran." Cassie's parents were out of town at a wedding, and her leaving would be up to Gran. But Cassie and Gran usually saw eye-to-eye. Gran was the only member of the Jones household who knew the whole truth about Cassie's daring adventures as a detective.

"Right. I'll call you back in ten minutes. Talk fast, and be very persuasive, please. Rod's trying to make light of this, but I know he's frightened.''

The word "frightened" echoed through Cassie's head as Alex hung up. A part of Cassie was scared, too. Investigating a mystery on a movie set involving a well-known rock star was serious business. But she was glad Alex had faith in her, and she had faith in herself. You are the "best," she often reminded herself. She'd go!

She crossed the hallway into the kitchen where her grandmother was waiting patiently over a cup of tea.

6

"Gran, Alex wants me to come to Hollywood," Cassie said. She glanced out the kitchen window and saw that Mel was safely out of earshot. "I'll be staying with her in her hotel room. You know it'll be the most luxurious hotel in the city."

"I'm not worried about your being with Alex," said Gran. "But why does she want you to come?" Gran's tone of voice suggested that she'd overheard some of Cassie's conversation.

"She needs some help with a problem. I don't know all the details. It involves an accident on the set of a movie."

" 'Problem.' 'Accident.' Those words worry me," said Gran, frowning. "I told your parents I'd look after you and Mel. But I suppose Hollywood *is* closer than England. There's probably some simple explanation for whatever is going on."

"Probably." Cassie smiled.

"Will you promise me, Cassie," said Gran, "that you'll stay close to Alexandra and not try to become a one-woman Scotland Yard?"

For Cassie this was an easy promise to make. She had no intention of foolishly placing herself in danger. "I promise to be careful, Gran."

At that moment Mel ran in from the yard. "Are you going to Hollywood, Cassie?" Mel asked excitedly. "Are you going to meet Rod Taggart?"

"It looks like I am," Cassie said.

"Promise me you'll memorize everything about

him,'' Melanie pleaded. ''What he wears, what he eats—and get his autograph.'' She clutched her heart. ''If I don't have that, I'll die!''

The telephone rang.

''Saved by the bell,'' Cassie teased. She ran for the phone, pleased she could tell Alex that Cassandra Best was on her way.

*T*he plane trip seemed to take forever, but at last Cassie arrived in Los Angeles. Alex was there to meet her and, after an affectionate hug, practically dragged her through the airport corridors. In no time at all they were headed onto the freeway.

From inside the sleek air-conditioned car, Cassie noticed the heavy layer of smog covering the city. The traffic was bumper to bumper, with thousands of cars ahead of them and behind them as far as the eye could see.

"How can you drive in this mess, Alex?" Cassie asked.

"Very carefully." Alex checked both her mirrors and changed lanes. "And I can't talk."

Cassie laughed, leaned back in the luxurious leather seat, and tried not to be nervous. This was some switch from the way the Joneses started vacation, cramped in their old station wagon, accompanied by fishing and camping gear.

They came to a dead stop, and Cassie asked, "Where'd you get this car?" They rode in a gleaming, silver gray Lincoln Continental.

"Majestic Pictures is trusting me with it while I'm here on assignment. Isn't it fabulous?"

"Sure is," said Cassie, noting that Alex looked fabulous, too. She had on a stone-washed denim miniskirt with a shiny magenta tank top. Over it, she wore a crisp white blouse knotted at her waist. The sleeves were neatly rolled to just below the elbow. A dozen bracelets clinked on her wrist. A black straw gaucho hat was perched on her dark, wavy hair. Cassie felt like the original hick from Ohio, sitting beside her. She'd dumped personal gear and a couple of outfits and shoes into a carry-on shoulder bag, but it would be fun to share some of Alex's clothes while she was here.

"Once we get off the freeway," said Alex, "I'll drive us along the scenic route. It's on the way to the studio, and it'll help you get the feel of Hollywood." Alex's deep-blue eyes sparkled. "Oh, I'm so glad to see you, Cassandra!"

"Me too, Alex—oh, look!" Cassie interrupted herself as she spotted a huge sign that read: HOLLYWOOD. "This is amazing. At lunchtime I was in Milltown, and now I'm actually here. *And* it's still only three o'clock."

"Have a good look at Tinseltown," said Alex a

few moments later. "And welcome to the Avenue of the Stars."

Cassie peered through the smoked-glass window. She could see gleaming gold-colored stars inlaid along the brownish-rose stone of the sidewalk.

"Rod's supposed to have a star named for him before the picture is over—*if* the film ever gets made," said Alex.

"Alex, what exactly is going on, anyway?"

"Be patient, Cassandra," Alex said. "I'll give you all the details when we get to the hotel."

Cassie decided to relax and enjoy the sights—for now.

"This is Hollywood and Vine—heard of that?" Alex again bubbled over with her own excitement. Spots of color in her cheeks contrasted with her peaches-and-cream complexion.

Cassie stared at the famous landmark corner. She expected to see glamorous stars strolling along in fancy clothing, but all she saw were tourists wearing sporty summer clothes and taking pictures with cameras hung from straps around their necks.

"There's Mann's Theatre." Alex pointed out the Chinese-style movie house. "It's famous because the stars' footprints are embedded in the cement out front."

"For a visitor, you've certainly learned a lot about Hollywood," Cassie said. "What's that?"

She peered out the window at what seemed to be

11

a huge mastodon's head rising out of a sticky black tar pool.

"It's only a model," Alex explained. "But I do admit I nearly drove the car into a lamppost the first time I saw it rising out of the pit. And the mastodon next to it looks like it wants to help its friend."

Cassie nodded, touched by the scene of the two helpless beasts being swallowed up by the tar. Tourists were lining up to get a closer view, their cameras poised and ready.

The traffic lights changed to green and the two girls left the La Brea Tar Pits behind them. Soon they were on a wider boulevard lined with exclusive homes. "Is this Beverly Hills?" Cassie asked, "or Bel Air?" She'd read about the stars' fabulous homes and seen photographs in magazines.

"Neither," said Alex, glancing at Cassie. "The stars live in palatial mansions. Wait till you see. I've already been to a party at an estate that could double for The Oaks." Alex's family lived at The Oaks, their mansion outside of London. "I'm sure there'll be another party or two while you're here."

"I can't wait," said Cassie excitedly.

They entered a winding private road that led up to the Hollywood Hills Hotel. "The cast and film crew are staying here," Alex said. "The hotel is a bit modern for my taste, but everyone else seems to like it."

More than a *bit* modern, thought Cassie, taking in

the sleek, luxurious hotel and magnificent grounds. After leaving the car with a parking attendant, the girls headed for the hotel entrance.

They walked through glass and chrome doors and into the bright, mirrored lobby. The floors were black marble, and Cassie saw her reflection everywhere.

"We'll just drop your things upstairs and get right over to the studio," said Alex, leading the way to the elevator.

The girls' suite was in the same style as the lobby, with a mirrored wall, track lighting, and lush, peach-colored carpeting. Across one wall stretched a plate-glass window with a breathtaking view of the city below.

"The view is even more spectacular at night," said Alex. "And now for the pièce de résistance," she added, dramatically flinging open another pair of doors.

The bathroom was all black marble, with brass fixtures. Right in the middle was a sunken, shell-shaped tub. Two thick, terry-cloth robes lay across the marble bench beside it.

"I wouldn't mind spending a few days here," Cassie observed aloud.

"California, you mean?" asked Alex.

Cassie smiled. "That, too, but I meant the tub."

Alex laughed. "Well, we're already late and I do want to fill you in on the case before we meet Rod at the studio."

Cassie was glad that Alex was finally ready to talk.

"It seems that someone's trying to get rid of Rod," Alex began. "I'm certain what's been happening isn't just accidental."

"What *has* been happening?" asked Cassie.

"Mishaps. Part of the set collapsed during one of Rod's scenes, and his safety cable snapped during filming of a difficult stunt. Then the brakes failed on Rod's prop car. He wasn't hurt in the crash, but everyone said he could've been seriously injured.

"You see," Alex went on, "Rod insists on doing his own stunts, even though his stunt double, Sky Bowman, was hired to do them for him."

"Why does Rod insist?" asked Cassie. "It sounds to me as if he's looking for trouble."

"Not at all," answered Alex. "You have to understand Rod. He grew up poor in Liverpool and ran around with a pretty rough crowd, even when he first started singing. It means a lot to him to follow through on his own."

"This is Rod's first movie, isn't it?" asked Cassie. "I read an article that said he was thinking of making a permanent career change from singing to acting."

Alex nodded. "That's right. I guess that's why he wants to prove he can do everything. Even stunts."

"Stunt work sounds dangerous," said Cassie. "Isn't it possible that the accidents are just accidents?"

"At first that's what I thought," said Alex. "But there have been so many unexplained incidents that everyone involved in the production is nervous. And now there's a rumor flying around the set that *Witches' Brew* is jinxed."

"Has anyone been directly involved in the accidents besides Rod?" asked Cassie.

"No, but there've been some close calls."

"Well, it certainly does look as if someone's trying to kill Rod—or at least frighten him off the picture," said Cassie. "Have you noticed anything else unusual about the production or about the cast or crew?"

"Not really," said Alex, thinking. "Oh, I don't know how important this is, but Rod's ex-girlfriend is his co-star."

"You mean Holly Chiswick?" asked Cassie.

"Then you know her?"

Cassie shook her head. "Just what I've read in magazines."

"Well, I'll bet you haven't read that Holly, although she speaks with a British accent, was born in Brooklyn, New York, and her real name is Molly Jenkins."

That surprised Cassie. "But I doubt I'll use that in my article," Alex went on. "It's all I can do to keep Tanya Grant at arm's length, making sure her stars' images aren't tarnished. Come to think

15

of it, though, she might not worry so much about Holly's.''

''Who's Tanya Grant?''

''She's production secretary on *Witches' Brew*. But she's also crazy about Rod. She and Holly can't stand each other.''

After they talked, the girls left the hotel and drove the short distance to the studio. Alex slowed for the huge wrought-iron gate that loomed before them. Above it was a wide arch over which was an enormous sign with gold-colored letters that read: MAJESTIC PICTURES.

Alex handed the uniformed guard a card and said, ''Alexandra Bennett and Cassandra Best. We're expected.''

The guard checked the list on his clipboard, then went inside a small cubicle and pressed the entrance button. The gate swung open to welcome them. Soon Alex was heading down a broad avenue that was as heavily populated by people as the freeway had been by cars. Cassie was fascinated by the crowds of actors and actresses strolling along or driving small motor carts. They were dressed in an incredible variety of costumes: cowboys, animals, aliens from outer space, and clowns.

On the lot where Alex moved into a parking space marked Reserved: A. Bennett, a small group of people dressed in long robes were waiting in front of a flat-roofed building marked Soundstage A. A red light above the entrance was on. The moment it went off, the person closest to the door pulled it open and, with the others, disappeared inside.

"You'll find the Majestic lot is a small city," Alex explained.

Cassie glanced around. This "small city" was bigger than the main shopping area in Milltown! And around every corner was a completely new scene. Down one block Cassie could see what looked like the main street of a frontier town, complete with saloon. Down another was a gleaming, futuristic village. And looming in the distance she recognized the space tower set for the recent science-fiction movie, *Cosmic Dawn*.

It was exactly what she'd expected a major studio to look like. The thought that everyone was working together to create movies gave Cassie a shiver of excitement, in spite of the heat.

Alex took the keys from the ignition and dropped them into her purse. "Come on. It's time to meet the cast."

The girls climbed the steps to Soundstage A just as the red light went on again.

"They're shooting," Alex explained as three bells sounded from inside.

When the red light over the entrance went out, Alex pulled open the heavy metal door. "Welcome to the *real* Hollywood," she said grandly.

Cassie stepped into the most enormous interior

17

she had ever seen. The soundstage was as long as a football field and as tall as an airplane hangar. Cameras, spotlights, and cranes towered above her like a forest of metal trees.

"Wow," said Cassie. "Is the entire production of *Witches' Brew* being shot on this soundstage?"

"Some of the exterior scenes will be shot outside on the studio lot," Alex answered. "But most will be filmed here."

Alex led Cassie on a tour past partially dismantled wood and cardboard sets. "Here's the graveyard set for the scene that was shot last week. And here's the cave set for the witches' coven scenes that will be shot in a day or two."

Cassie peered at what looked like a mound of rough gray stones. She reached out her hand to touch one and was surprised to find that the rock was soft, like Styrofoam. "What's this movie about, anyway?"

"Rod Taggart plays a rock star who finds out his girlfriend—that's Holly Chiswick—belongs to a witches' coven," Alex answered. "He rescues her, then discovers he's stirred up all the powers of darkness. Witches, warlocks, and things that go bump in the night start showing up at his concerts, until . . . Well, I don't want to give away the ending," Alex said with a laugh.

"Do you think it'll be a hit?" Cassie asked.

"Should be. It's got all the right ingredients—

music, monsters, and mayhem. *Plus* the best-looking leading man on either side of the Atlantic.''

The girls kept walking toward the sound of voices. ''Today,'' Alex continued, ''you're just in time to meet everyone before the shooting starts.''

They came to a brightly lit set of a luxurious living room and lobby with a long staircase that wound up into thin air.

Cassie noticed immediately that only three people on the set were costumed and made up. The others, at least a dozen men and women, were wearing jeans and T-shirts. Some were nailing rug corners to the floor of the set. Others were moving enormous lights, and still others were winding cables above or behind furniture. One girl was placing tape marks at various spots on the rug.

Alex said, ''Come on. There's Rod.''

They stepped carefully over long electrical cords and made their way to the cleared area where they found three canvas chairs. Rod Taggart rose from his chair to greet them. To Cassie, it seemed as though the familiar-looking poster from her bedroom wall had come to life. Rod was incredibly handsome.

Wavy, dark brown hair curled behind his ears and one lock fell over his forehead. His brown eyes were hypnotic. There was an energy around him that was like a sign flashing STAR! STAR!

This isn't happening, thought Cassie excitedly. This can't be Rod Taggart in the flesh! She was sorry

19

not to have changed from her tan skirt and green tank top into something more sophisticated.

"Rod, this is my American cousin from Ohio," Alex said, introducing Cassie in a way Cassie hadn't expected. "You remember, I told you about her. She's an actress at a playhouse there," Alex added, giving Rod a knowing look, which he returned.

Cassie straightened her shoulders and held out her hand. You are the "best," she reminded herself. To Rod she said casually, "Hi, I'm Cassandra Best."

Rod took Cassie's hand and continued to hold it. His smile could have melted Arctic ice. "And I'm Rod. Alex told me she was going to drag you away from your busy schedule back East. She had to do some fancy coaxing, I'd imagine."

Was he kidding? thought Cassie. She smiled at Rod. "Oh, not really. We're between shows, and I enjoy traveling, meeting new people." Cassie didn't dare look at Alex. They'd both burst out laughing.

Rod released Cassie's hand abruptly as two girls joined them.

One was a blond. Cassie recognized her as Holly Chiswick. She'd read about the fabulous starlet whom the newspapers had called the "British Bombshell." Holly certainly lived up to her name. Her hair was the color and texture of spun gold, with not a single strand out of place. Her blue eyes were the color of the sea, and her eyelashes were double-thick. Her teeth were perfect. Her manicure was perfect. In fact, thought Cassie, Holly Chiswick herself is perfect, maybe too perfect to be real.

Alex, at ease with both Rod and Holly, made the introductions, and the Bombshell held out a long, slim hand. "It's so awfully good to meet you, Cassandra," Holly purred in her British accent.

"I'm Tanya Grant," said the much more real-looking and real-sounding girl standing alongside Holly. She certainly presented a contrast.

Tanya's hair was caramel brown. She wore it short and tousled. Everything about her seemed natural, and Cassie liked her at once. Holly seemed "costumed" in a white suede pants suit with silver sandals, but Tanya was simply dressed in jeans and a red T-shirt with black letters that spelled out WITCHES' BREW on the front and MAJESTIC on the back. Her shoes were cowboy boots.

"Hey, Rod," said a man coming up to the group just then. "Marty's called a meeting in his office. He wants to go over a few last-minute changes in the scene before we shoot." He saw Cassie and smiled, although in doing so, the cigar he'd been puffing on almost fell from between his yellow-stained teeth.

The man acted important, but looked just the opposite. A straw hat covered an obviously bald head. The gaudiest shirt Cassie had ever seen barely covered his potbelly. A khaki vest didn't meet in the middle.

"Jeff Ryan," said Alex, "meet Cassandra Best."

21

"You must be the Best Gal," Jeff quipped.

"Jeff's always inventing puns," explained Tanya.

"Yeah," said Rod. "And he's the executive producer on this flick, so we've all got to laugh whether the puns are funny or not."

"I'll laugh," Alex said, "but I don't understand this one. Best Gal?"

"Cassandra's name," explained Jeff. "The head electrician on a film is called Best Boy."

"Oh, an in-joke." Alex circled Cassie's waist and hugged her. "Well, she is my best friend." Alex winked at Cassie and Cassie smiled.

"She has a lovely smile," said Holly. "You may have to give her a part, Jeff."

The producer laughed, and this time the cigar did fall. He ground it out with the heel of his shoe, then picked up the butt and dropped it into a nearby garbage can. Reaching into the pocket of his safari vest, he pulled out another cigar. It was wrapped in cellophane, which he removed. He slid off the paper ring and handed it to Cassie.

"If you need anything, Best Gal," he joked, "give me a ring."

Cassie took the ring and laughed.

Then Jeff turned to Rod and said, "Marty called the meeting for five minutes from now."

"Right," said Rod. "Ladies, if you'll excuse me—"

Suddenly, there was a thundering crack as a bank

of lights broke loose from the ceil: plummeting to the ground. Cassie, lightning speed, pulled Alex out of th time to avoid their being hit.

The small group stared, speechless. The heavy metal bar had fallen directly onto one of the canvas chairs, smashing it to bits. It was the chair labeled with Rod's name, the one he had been sitting in when Cassie arrived on the set.

Chapter
3

*T*anya Grant flung her arms around Rod. Visibly shaken, she cried, "You could have been killed!"

If anything, Rod seemed angry. "Well, I wasn't, so there's nothing to get upset about."

Cassie glanced at Alex, who was trembling, too. Holly Chiswick patted her hair to be sure it was still in place. But Jeff Ryan suggested, "Maybe we should call the police."

"To report that some lights fell?" asked Rod.

"No 'maybe' about it, Jeff," said Tanya. "Let's do it. And someone ought to tell Marty why Rod's not at his script meeting."

There was no need. A tall man with curly gray hair and pale-blue eyes approached the group. He wore a black turtleneck over black slacks. His air of authority told Cassie he was the director.

"What happened?" Marty Ingram exclaimed. "One of the grips came to get me. He said there's been another incident."

24

"Accident," corrected Rod.

"I told Rod we should call the police," said Jeff.

"No way," said Rod, looking as if he wanted to escape all the attention surrounding him.

"What about studio security?" asked Cassie. "They'd understand the need to investigate quietly, without inviting any negative publicity."

The gray-haired man in black turned to her. "That's a good idea, young lady. Who are you? I'm Marty Ingram."

"Cassandra Best," Cassie answered, putting out her hand.

"Now I remember," said Marty, shaking Cassie's hand. "You're Alex's American cousin, aren't you? She said you would be here today."

"Yes." Cassie looked at Alex as if to say, Just how many people have you told about your "cousin"? Alex smiled and shrugged. "I've come West to visit family," Cassie said smoothly.

"Well, that's what we've got here, Cass," said Marty. "One big happy family. So just make yourself at home."

"Thanks, Mr. Ingram—"

"Marty. We all use first names on my set, Cass."

But does he have to shorten mine? thought Cassie. And someone in the family seems to be less than happy about Rod being in this film. Cassie planned on finding out who right away. "Marty, I'd like to ask—"

25

"Later, Cass, later. We're way behind schedule here." He turned to Tanya. "See if we're ready to shoot. The rest of you—Holly, Jeff, Rod—come into my office. I've got a few things to go over, and incidents, accidents—whatever—can't get in our way." Marty Ingram's voice was businesslike.

"But Mr. Ing—Marty," said Cassie.

"Can't take the time to answer questions right now, Cass. Tell you what. I'm having a few people over to the house tomorrow. Nothing fancy—just sit around the pool, eat a few munchies. Why don't you join us? We can talk then. Alex, you come, too. Jeff can pick you both up at your hotel."

"The studio has been kind enough to supply me with a car," said Alex.

"Marty lives in the hills, Alex," said Jeff. "You'd never find the house. Took me two years before I could find it, but I finally figured out all the twists and turns. I'll pick you girls up at noon. And as exec producer, I won't take no for an answer. Okay?"

Alex shrugged and looked at Cassie. "Okay," agreed Cassie, "noon it is."

The others left for Marty's office, which was at the rear of the soundstage with the other executive offices and the dressing rooms. Cassie planned to stay behind. "I want to have a better look at those stage lights that fell, Alex," she said when they were alone.

"Okay," Alex agreed. "I'm going to sit in on the

meeting to get some background information for my article. I'll meet you later. Anything I can do in the meantime?''

Cassie thought, then said, ''I'd like to talk with someone from studio security. Do you know any of the guards?''

''Yes,'' answered Alex. ''Consider it done.'' She left.

Moments later, as Cassie was examining the frayed ends of rope that had allowed the bank of stage lights to fall, a uniformed man in his sixties came up to her.

''Looks more than frayed, doesn't it?'' the man asked.

''It sure does,'' answered Cassie, having reached the same conclusion. The rope looked cut. ''Can you tell me who might have had access to the area in the past half hour or so? Oh, by the way, I'm Cassandra Best.''

''I know. Miss Bennett told me. I'm Hank. But I'm afraid I can't help you, Miss Best. Everyone has access when a movie's shooting.''

''Hmmm, then tell me this. Rod's chair had his name on it, but does he always sit there after a take? Are the chairs always in the same position? Who'd know that sort of thing?''

Hank shook his head. ''Answer's still the same. People are creatures of habit. There's usually a long wait between setups. Some of the actors return to their dressing rooms. But Mr. Taggart's habit is to fall into his chair and close his eyes. Says his dressing room is too bright and too hot. But everyone on the set knows that habit, you see?''

Cassie nodded. ''When you say everyone, Hank, how many people do you mean?''

Hank scratched his balding head. ''Well, depends on the difficulty of the shot. But you're talking about grips, electricians, carpenters, assistants—and their assistants—not to mention the actors, extras, and union reps. It gets pretty crowded around here.''

''I imagine it does.'' And no one pays any attention to anyone else, Cassie added to herself. Each person has a job to do and goes about doing it, not questioning anyone else's actions.

She checked the backs of the other canvas chairs. From the names, it seemed that Holly Chiswick sat on Rod's left, and Sky Bowman's chair was on the right.

''I've met Holly Chiswick,'' she said to Hank. ''But where is Mr. Bowman this afternoon?''

''He's off on a break. He's Mr. Taggart's stunt-double. But Mr. Taggart likes to do his own stunts, so there's not much work for Mr. Bowman on this picture.'' Hank winked. ''Of course, he's here most of the time anyway, but that's for a different reason. Miss Chiswick. You know, the Brit Bombshell.''

''Really?'' Cassie filed the tidbit of information.

"Yep. If the Bombshell is anywhere nearby, chances are Sky Bowman isn't far away."

Cassie made another mental note to find out if Rod's stunt-double had been nearby when the stage lights fell. Because Holly Chiswick certainly had been.

Hank left Cassie turning over the facts she'd gathered and questions she wanted to ask. Before she knew it, Rod, Holly, and Jeff returned to the set. Other personnel began to appear, each going about his or her specialized job.

Lights were tested and retested. Rod's stand-in, an extra who was close to Rod in height, weight, and coloring, walked back and forth while a woman held a meter up to his face and then scribbled notes on a pad.

Tanya Grant, who wore a stopwatch on a long chain around her neck, came up to Cassie just as Alex joined her. "You'll find things going slowly around here for the rest of the day. We're shooting a couple of pages without much action. If you like, I can arrange for someone to show you around. More personal than the usual kind of studio tour."

"I'd love it," said Cassie.

Holly Chiswick was standing within earshot. "Oh, don't bother with a studio guide, Tanya. Marty says I'm free for another hour or more. I'll show Cassandra the sights."

"Terrific," answered Cassie. "Alex, you'll come, too, won't you?"

"Well, I—"

"We might even learn something," said Cassie, trying to make it sound as though she were referring to movies. What she hoped was to learn more about the attempts that had been made to harm Rod Taggart.

Apparently Alex got the message. "Sure, I can't think of anything I'd rather do. Holly, lead the way."

They were joined outside the soundstage exit by a young man who could be no one but Sky Bowman. Cassie noticed that Holly lit up like a neon sign when she saw him. She wondered if the Brit Bombshell had fallen for Sky because of his strong resemblance to her ex-boyfriend. Even Sky's hair was like Rod's, down to the stray lock that fell over his forehead as he talked.

Sky Bowman was friendly and outgoing, which made Cassie wonder why Rod Taggart had such a magnetizing effect on everyone when Sky didn't. It must be in the stars, she mused. Then she cringed. I'd better watch it. Jeff Ryan's puns may be contagious.

"We don't want to interrupt any film shooting," Sky was saying, "so we'll visit the TV stages. The shows are on hiatus right now, so we can poke around and nobody will mind."

He led them inside a building filled with science-fiction sets. Huge monsters made of papier-mâché leaned lazily against Styrofoam walls painted to look like precious alabaster and marble.

"Do you ever watch *Orbit?*" asked Holly, her arm entwined possessively through Sky's.

"No," answered Cassie. "Why?"

"Well, on that show Sky isn't just a stunt-double. He's one of the leads."

"Past tense," offered Sky. "The show's been canceled." To Alex and Cassie he said, "That's why I took the job in *Witches' Brew*. Till something better comes along."

"It would come sooner," said Holly, "if Rod were out of the picture."

Cassie and Alex looked at each other, and Holly said quickly, "Hey, wait a minute, I didn't mean *this* picture. I'd never do anything to harm Rod. And I'm not still in love with him, no matter what the newspapers say."

"What do they say?" asked Cassie.

"Oh, stupid things about my accepting this picture to get Rod back." Holly leaned over to kiss Sky's cheek. "I couldn't care less about Rod now."

Cassie watched Holly closely. Was Holly sincere or was she just acting? Cassie wasn't sure. She'd try to find out more about Holly later.

After they'd toured the *Orbit* sets, Alex said, "Sky, I don't know about Cassandra, but I'd love to see the costumes worn by the stars in really famous old movies. You know, Dorothy's gingham pinafore from *The Wizard of Oz*, or Scarlett's ball gowns from *Gone With the Wind*.''

''Wrong studio, Alex,'' he said. ''Majestic specializes in horror films and science fiction, with an occasional western. But tell me—'' He paused dramatically outside a door, then flung it open. ''What do you think of . . . this?''

Cassie's mouth fell open at the sight of a huge group of realistic-looking animals peering at the four humans standing in the doorway. Gorillas, lions, bears, giraffes, and elephants were only a few of the vast room's occupants.

Sky pointed to an angry-looking lion and said, ''In my first film, Leo there charged me head-on. I didn't have to *act* scared. I was so frightened that I went up a tree! That was when we all discovered I was good at stunts, especially climbing ones.''

Including stunts like climbing the catwalks leading to the banks of overhead stage lights? wondered Cassie. She felt Alex's elbow nudge her as they left the building. They'd obviously been thinking the same thing.

Next they visited the special-effects department, which fascinated Cassie.

''This is where they're making the dancing skeletons that appear in the film during one of the concert scenes," said Holly. She showed Cassie and Alex the miniature plastic skeletons.

"How do the skeletons come alive?" asked Cassie.

"Through stop-motion photography," Sky answered. "The animators move the skeletons a fraction of an inch, photograph them, and then repeat the procedure. They're lucky to get five seconds of film a day."

"What a time-consuming process!" Alex exclaimed.

"Anything for realism," said Holly. "Soon these skeletons will be able to break-dance as well as Rod."

They completed the tour. Then, while Sky and Holly returned to Soundstage A, Alex and Cassie strolled about the lot on their own.

"Marty's party will be great fun," said Alex.

"That reminds me," said Cassie. "Do you have an extra swimsuit I can borrow?"

"I packed several. I'm sure one of them will fit you."

"Great."

"Let's catch the next scene on the set," Alex suggested.

The filming fascinated Cassie at first: the master shot, then the different angles; Marty reminding the actors to "save the emotions for the close-ups." Cassie imagined what it would be like to play the scene herself.

But by the eleventh take of the identical scene, Cassie found a tiny yawn escaping and her stomach growling. She was relieved when the assistant director called, "One hour for dinner. Everybody back at seven."

"Let's go," said Cassie. "I'm starving. I just realized I haven't eaten since breakfast."

"You always forget to eat when you're on a case," teased Alex.

"And you always get grouchy when you don't have your tea," Cassie teased back.

The girls had dinner at the commissary, a huge cafeteria where everyone working on the lot had their meals. Alex complained about Americans not knowing how to make a decent cup of tea, but she drank two cups anyway.

"Let's get back," said Cassie, hurrying to finish her Coke. "I don't want to miss anything. This is fascinating, Alex!"

Back on the *Witches' Brew* set, the crew had begun to prepare for the next scene.

"Where's Rod?" asked Alex.

"He's in his dressing room," answered an assistant.

"Let's talk to him," suggested Cassie. "And I have some questions I want to ask Tanya when we see her."

"She's usually with Rod. Goes everywhere with him," continued the assistant.

The girls got directions from the assistant, then headed down the corridor toward Rod's dressing room. Just outside his door, Cassie noticed a large square message board. On it hung the day's shooting schedule along with miscellaneous personal notes that had been tacked on by cast or crew members. Someone named Stew was desperate for a ride up to San Francisco. A girl named Tracey offered ''all her worldly possessions'' for the return of her favorite cat. Cassie smiled, then she and Alex went inside.

Tanya was with Rod now.

At first Cassie wondered if they'd had a fight. The production secretary seemed upset about something. Then Cassie saw a crumpled note beside the mirror on Rod's dressing table. Tanya reached for it, just as his hand grabbed her wrist.

''Tanya, I told you—it's nothing,'' he said angrily.

''Rod, for heaven's sake,'' cried Tanya.

''It's just a silly prank.'' Rod jumped up and paced the room, sweeping the piece of paper to the floor.

''What is?'' asked Cassie, closing the door.

''Someone left Rod a threatening note,'' said Tanya.

''It's not, Tanya!'' Rod said, pounding his fist on the wall. ''Will you leave it alone?''

''No, Rod, I won't! Why won't you show it to me?''

"Because it's a stupid joke, that's why!"

Tanya stared at him for a moment, her cheeks flushed with fury. "Fine," she said, clenching her fists. "If that's the way you want it." Tanya headed for the door, close to tears. Alex stepped aside, letting her go. Tanya pulled the door open and slammed it loudly behind her.

In the silence that followed, Cassie reached down and scooped up the crumpled ball of paper. Alex moved to stand beside her as Cassie opened the note, smoothed the paper, and read the typewritten message:

> *Just to shed a little light on the subject:*
> *The bigger they are, the harder they fall.*

"You know why I'm here, Rod, don't you?" Cassie asked.

Rod nodded, looking shaken now that Tanya had left the room. "What do you make of it all?" he asked. "It isn't just a joke, is it?"

"I don't think so," Cassie said. "And that bank of lights falling was no accident, either."

Rod sat down and ran a hand through his hair. "I know. The note makes that perfectly clear. This is so strange. I'll be honest with you, it's really starting to get to me. These incidents are getting more and more frequent, and deadlier every time. Someone's out to hurt me, that's for sure. What I can't figure out is *why!*"

"Well, have you got any enemies?" Cassie prodded. "Someone who's tried to hurt you before?"

Rod shook his head. "No one that I can think of. I'm a really nice guy," he said, throwing her his famous smile.

"Have you gotten any other notes before this one?"

"Not a one, have I, Alex?" Alex shook her head by way of agreement. "And I don't have a clue about who left this one. Anybody could have done it. Anybody at all. It was tacked on the studio message board right outside this room, and it had my name on it."

Alex took the note from Cassie and looked at it. " 'The bigger they are . . .' " she said. "Do you think that refers to the big bank of stage lights?"

"Either that," answered Cassie, "or the bigger the star . . ."

No one wanted to finish the sentence.

*A*n assistant knocked on the door and announced, "It's a wrap for today. No call tomorrow."

"We'd better go, Cassandra," said Alex. "They close the soundstage pretty fast when they're through for the day. Otherwise, they run the risk of going into overtime." She looked at Rod. "Coming?" she asked him. "We could give you a lift back to the hotel."

"No thanks," Rod said with that killer smile of his. "Tanya's pretty upset. I'd better go calm her down."

"Right. Bye, then," said Alex.

"Oh, Rod," Cassie broke in. "May I keep this for a while?" she asked, holding up the note.

He shrugged. "If you want. It doesn't matter to me."

But Cassie knew it did matter to him. In spite of his courage, Rod Taggart appeared shaken.

Cassie pocketed the note and said, "See you tomorrow, then."

The girls said goodnight to Rod, then headed for the parking lot.

"I'm so worried about Rod," said Alex when they'd settled into the car. "Do you have any idea who could have sent that note?" She pulled out of the lot and headed for the hotel.

"I'd have to guess, Alex. It could have been anyone."

Cassie thought back to what Hank, the security guard, had said to her earlier. People here know everyone's habits. For instance, she thought, everyone on the set knows Jeff's obsession with bad puns. If whoever wrote that note wanted it to look as if Jeff sent it, he or she would write in some puns like "shed a little light." Aloud she said, "The note doesn't reveal much about whoever wrote it, except that they're definitely after Rod."

"I guess you're right, Cassie. What do you plan to do now?" Alex sounded tired and discouraged.

Cassie felt only tired. "Get some sleep. There's nothing we can do tonight."

The following morning Cassie awoke to find a room-service cart at the foot of her bed. On the cart was breakfast for two: scrambled eggs, a basket of warm muffins, and a pitcher of fresh orange juice.

"Where did this come from?" asked Cassie, rubbing her eyes awake, stretching, reveling in the luxury of the crisp sheets and oversized downy pillows.

"From my getting up while you were off in the Land of Nod," said Alex, who was already dressed.

She wore a long man-tailored shirt of gauzy blue cotton, with a darker blue bikini underneath it. Over a chair arm was a candy-striped bikini with a matching skirt for Cassie.

"I've always wanted a sister I could share clothes with," Cassie remarked as she put on the suit. "Especially *her* clothes."

"Someday I'll show up in Ohio and commandeer all your blue jeans," Alex jokingly replied. She poured herself a cup of tea.

After breakfast, the girls went down to the lobby. Jeff Ryan arrived at noon sharp, wearing a straw hat and a green-and-orange Hawaiian shirt. He stepped out of a chauffeur-driven white stretch limousine.

Who needs a pool? thought Cassie when she saw the limo. We could fit the entire cast and crew of *Witches' Brew* in the backseat and have the party in here!

Jeff climbed in after Alex and Cassie and asked, "Comfy, girls?"

"Yes, thank you. Just fine," Cassie answered.

Alex whispered under her breath, "It's a bit tacky, if you ask me. Still, I do wonder what's on television." She flicked on the built-in color set.

"Hey, girls, you don't mind if I light up, do you?"

asked Jeff. Without waiting for a reply, he took a cigar from his jacket pocket. As he had done before, he removed the cellophane wrapper and the paper cigar ring. "Here," he said, dropping the ring into Cassie's hand, "for your collection." He lit the cigar and immediately the backseat filled with smoke. Both girls began to cough uncontrollably.

"Jeff, may we open a window?" asked Alex. "It's a bit stuffy in here."

"Yeah, sure." He pressed a button, and the black-shaded windows slid away. Rolling green hills appeared on the horizon. Palm trees lined the road, and the air was warm and breezy.

Cassie was admiring the beautiful scenery when Jeff asked, "So, Cassandra, what do you think of Tinseltown?"

"It's like one big movie set!" she answered.

"No place like it! I'd bet the odds in Vegas that anyone who visits here never wants to leave. Except Rod, maybe."

"Why do you say that?" asked Cassie.

"Well, being under the spotlights didn't go to his head in England—he fell for them here!" Jeff's laughter at his own pun turned into a coughing spasm, and Cassie had to pound him on the back so he wouldn't choke.

The limo turned onto a private road that rose higher and higher into the winding hills. Cassie's ears began to pop.

"We're almost there," said Jeff, pointing to what looked like a tiny speck on the top of a mountain. The speck grew larger until at last the driver made a final turn and even Alex, who was accustomed to luxurious surroundings, said, "It's magnificent!"

Jeff, his cigar hanging from between his teeth, punned, "Not magnificent, girls—*majestic!*"

This time he'd used the perfect word. The driver jumped out from behind the wheel and came to open the rear passenger door. Cassie stepped onto a terra-cotta tiled walk that led to the three-story Spanish-style *hacienda*. The house was made of white stucco trimmed with black wrought iron and dark wood. Several fountains spouted water from bronze nymphs, turtles, and dolphins. There were hedged-in gardens on three separate levels, each visible from the circular driveway entrance. Brightly colored flowers perfumed the clear, clean air that was high enough to be above the Hollywood smog.

"Welcome to my humble abode," called Marty Ingram, coming to greet them. He was wearing bathing trunks and his hair was wet. "Come on out to the pool. The water's just right."

He led Jeff, Alex, and Cassie through a maze of shrubs and rustling trees. The sparkling blue water in the Olympic-sized pool shone like diamonds. A few people were actually swimming, but most of the guests in the water were either floating on colorful rafts or playfully splashing each other.

"Hey, there, look out below!" called Rod Taggart from above.

Cassie looked up and saw him do a perfect somersault dive into the deep water.

"He's good enough to qualify for the Olympics," she said, watching from the side of the pool, admiring his even tan and his muscular arms and legs.

"Yeah, well, he could get himself killed, too," said Jeff, relighting his cigar. "Of course, that wouldn't be in his best interest, would it? Maybe he could just get *almost* killed. We'd make a good audience, wouldn't we, standing here as witnesses?"

Cassie and Alex looked at one another, and then Cassie asked, "What are you talking about?"

Jeff shrugged. "Oh, I don't know. But if Rod's been staging his little accidents, it could mean a lot of publicity for him, even if the picture gets canceled—which is likely to happen if we continue to shoot over budget and behind schedule."

"I don't understand," said Alex.

"Neither do I, Jeff," said Cassie. "Rod's the one who hasn't wanted any of these mishaps reported. He's the one who's trying to avoid the publicity, isn't he?"

"Yeah. Maybe like Br'er Rabbit. Remember him? 'Please, oh please, don't throw me in the briar patch'?" To Alex he said, "Maybe in British families the kids didn't read those stories."

43

"Perhaps that's why I still don't understand," said Alex.

Jeff's face turned into a scowl. "Br'er Rabbit was only pretending when he begged not to be thrown into the briar patch. What he wanted was the opposite."

"To be thrown *into* the briars?" asked Alex.

"Sure! So who knows, maybe Rod wants everyone to think he doesn't want any publicity about his accidents, when in fact that's exactly what he *does* want."

Cassie had been listening and trying to find a motive. "Jeff, there would have to be a reason. Why would he do something like that?"

Chewing on his cigar, the executive producer answered, "Beats me." Then, waving to two other men in Hawaiian shirts, he said, "Speaking of publicity, gotta greet the press. Take a dip. Have fun. It's too hot to think."

But Cassie was deep in thought. "There has to be a reason, Alex," she said. "Because if Rod doesn't have one, someone may be going to a lot of trouble to make it seem as if he does. Maybe someone *else* wants him to suffer the bad publicity."

The girls were in the pool when Holly Chiswick arrived with Sky Bowman. Cassie marveled at the way the actress walked in her four-inch-high heels.

"I don't think I could even stand in those," she whispered to Alex.

"It's Hollywood," said Alex.

At that moment, Marty yelled, "Food time! C'mon inside the patio! Munchies for everyone!"

The girls climbed out of the pool and dried themselves off. Cassie wrapped her skirt around her and knotted it at the waist. Alex slipped into her overshirt. Then they joined the other guests.

A buffet table had been set up, and on it were gleaming silver platters and bowls filled with chipped ice and heaped with sumptuous delicacies. Cassie's eyes roamed over lobster and shrimp and caviar, individual cheese tarts, and a dozen different kinds of salad. Then, from behind, she heard Tanya Grant say, "Have a peek at the dessert cart."

The cart was just as lavishly arranged with an assortment of pastries. For a moment Cassie felt a mad urge to try one of everything. After all, she wasn't invited to a Hollywood party every day.

But she wasn't working on a case every day, either. With an inward sigh, she took only small samplings of several different seafoods and a slice of strawberry mousse pie. When she saw Marty Ingram sitting in the shade of the nearest palm tree, Cassie grabbed the chance to have a few words with him. So, instead of joining Alex and Tanya at one of the tables, she walked over to the empty chaise beside the director.

"May I join you?" she asked.

"Be my guest, Cass," he said, pulling apart the delicate meat of a lobster claw.

"This is really quite a party," said Cassie. "Do you do this often?"

"Usually I wait till a film I'm directing is ready to wrap," Marty replied between bites, "but with *Witches' Brew*, if I wait for that, we may wind up never having the party, so I figured—"

"Excuse me," said Cassie, "but is the film in danger of closing down or of not being completed?"

"Well, Cass," said Marty, "these constant delays are costing a fortune."

"By delays you mean . . ."

"I mean anything that holds up production. Every person you see on a film set, from the star on down to the person who refills the coffee machine, belongs to a different union. And they all get paid whether the cameras are rolling or not. Moviemaking is a very expensive business."

"But isn't a movie production insured against delays and mishaps? Accidents, too? I think it's called an insurance bond." Cassie recalled having read a magazine article on the subject.

"Sure," answered Marty, "but an insurance bond can get canceled. The insurance company, our production company, we're all in business to make money. But no insurers are going to cover an accident they know is going to happen."

Cassie wanted to ask more, but Marty Ingram had eaten all the food on his plate, and now he stood up and said, "It's my turn to ask you to excuse me, Cass. I've only finished my first course. See you."

Both Cassie and Alex were relaxing after the delicious meal. They were stretched out on cabana chairs in the shade of a huge yellow sun umbrella, when they heard shouting.

Cassie sat up and opened her eyes to see Rod Taggart and Jeff Ryan, who had both changed from their swimming trunks into slacks and sport shirts. They were arguing loudly at poolside. Tanya Grant was on the diving board, but instead of following through with the jump she'd just begun, she climbed down the ladder and rushed over to the two men.

Rod yelled, "Tanya, this is between Jeff and me. Stay out of it."

Tanya stepped back from them and looked around until she saw Marty. Cassie watched as Tanya went to the director, and Jeff Ryan muttered something under his breath.

It was something only Rod could hear, but it seemed to anger him even more. He lunged toward Jeff. For a few seconds, the two men wrestled furiously on the edge of the pool.

Marty Ingram and another guest ran over to stop the fight. But before they could get there, Rod cried

47

out, "One of these days, Ryan, you'll go too far, and you'll regret it!"

Jeff Ryan's fist thrust suddenly into Rod's stomach and sent him falling backward into the pool. Water splashed on everyone who had gathered to watch the scene.

Rod came up shaking his head and sputtering, "Ryan—you—you—" His rage wouldn't allow him to form the words.

"Good thing for him it was the deep water," said Sky Bowman, who was standing with an arm around Holly's waist. "If he'd landed on the steps at the other end, it might have been *the* end. His."

"Well, you know the old saying," Cassie heard Holly reply. "The bigger they are, the harder they fall."

The words on Rod's note!

"About that remark you just made, Holly," said Cassie. "You said the bigger they are—"

"Sure," interrupted Holly. "Rod made an awfully big splash, wouldn't you say?"

Yes, thought Cassie. I would say that.

She looked back toward Rod. Friends were helping him out of the pool, and Jeff Ryan was nervously lighting his umpteenth cigar as he approached the girls.

"What were you and Rod fighting about?" asked Cassie.

"Business," Jeff muttered. "None of anybody else's."

"You both looked really angry, Jeff," said Cassie.

"Yeah, well remember, this is movies with a capital *M*. Looks can be deceiving."

"But surely—"

"Curiosity killed the cat," said Jeff, cutting her off.

50

"C'mon, Cassandra," urged Alex, yanking Cassie by the arm, "let's have another swim."

"I'm going to find the bathroom," said Cassie. "This cat is also curious about Marty Ingram's house. I'll just be a minute." Cassie headed up the tiled walk and entered the enormous mansion.

Her mouth fell open when she saw the living room off the main center hallway. The ceiling was more than two stories high. A huge round wrought-iron chandelier hung directly overhead. It looked like some torturing device left in a dungeon after the Spanish Inquisition.

One entire wall was covered with engraved medieval armor and weapons. The opposite wall was a gallery of life-sized oil paintings in ornately carved gilt frames.

The floor under Cassie's bare feet was made of stone, and the furniture, while handsomely crafted of heavy wood and trimmed in antique leather, somehow made the entire room look more like a movie set than a living room. Cassie marveled that anyone, including Marty Ingram, could possibly "live" here.

"Looking for something?" asked a voice from the doorway behind her.

Cassie jumped.

There stood one of the young waiters who had been serving food and lemonade out on the patio. Like the others, he wore a red *Witches' Brew* T-shirt.

The waiter said again, "Are you looking for something?"

"Yes," answered Cassie. "The bathroom. Can you point me in the right direction?"

He shrugged. "I would, but I don't know the house very well. I'm just working today to help a friend who got a call to shoot a TV commercial. I'm really an actor." Smiling, he asked, "Are you in the business, too?"

"In a way," Cassie answered. "Listen, my friend is waiting for me at the pool, so—"

"Okay. Maybe we'll bump into each other on Marty's next picture. At least now we know where it's set."

"We do?" asked Cassie.

"Sure," said the actor-waiter. "Everybody knows Marty redecorates the ground floor of the house as soon as one of his pictures wraps. My friend told me that last month this place looked like a witches' den. And then Marty started shooting *Witches' Brew*. So I guess this Spanish torture chamber tells it all."

He did a quick flamenco dance step and, bowing low, said, *"Adios, señorita!"*

Cassie smiled and started down the hall.

The first three bathrooms she found were occupied. Imagine! she thought, recalling the early-morning wait outside the Joneses' single upstairs bathroom at home, especially if Melanie got there first!

Cassie had explored most of the ground floor in her search. She'd passed the vast dining room. Banquet hall was more like it. Again, the furnishings were Spanish, in keeping with Marty's upcoming picture. Hammered sconces and wrought-iron candelabras with candles rising three feet high stood against or hung from every wall.

The cool, ceramic tiles felt good under Cassie's bare feet. But now her toes brushed against something on the floor.

Someone had dropped a book of matches with a cowboy boot and spur embossed on the silver cover. As Cassie turned it slightly to see the detail of the design, the boot and spur disappeared, and in their place were rainbow-colored letters that spelled out a name: THE SILVER SPUR CASINO. Below, smaller letters spelled out: LAS VEGAS, NEVADA. The slightest movement of the matchbook made the writing vanish and the boot and spur reappear.

Cassie had never seen this kind of matchbook before, and since the matches inside were gone, she decided to keep the book as a souvenir of her first Hollywood party. Dropping it into the pocket of her wraparound skirt, she continued down the hall.

The door to a room on the right was slightly ajar. It was open just enough for Cassie to see a mirror, and in its reflection, the corner of a study. She recognized Marty Ingram's voice. He wasn't near the mirror, though, so she couldn't see him.

She wouldn't have stopped if it hadn't been for the director's words. He was obviously speaking into a telephone, because no one in the room was replying to him.

"I told you I'll come up with the money!" he shouted. "But I need more time! Look, I'm taking care of it, but there's nothing else I can do right now, so you'll have to let me handle it! And don't call me here again!"

He slammed the receiver down hard, and Cassie heard his chair creak. She also heard footsteps on the tile floor. There was someone else in the room, and that person was coming toward the door.

Toward her.

They'll know I eavesdropped! she thought, quickly glancing across the hall in search of a door. Any door would do.

She heard noises coming from one of the rooms, so she turned the knob and ducked inside.

"Hey, there! C'mon in!" called two guests. She hadn't met them before, but Cassie remembered having seen them on the set, so she knew they must be connected with *Witches' Brew*.

They were sitting in the largest Jacuzzi Cassie had ever seen. It took up two-thirds of the entire Spanish-tiled room and was even bigger than the backseat of Jeff Ryan's stretch limo.

"Don't be shy!" the girl called to Cassie. "The water's terrific!"

It looked too tempting to resist—and was a good place where she could duck out of sight.

Cassie unknotted her skirt and dropped it on the wicker table that was piled high with plush, velvety towels in jewel-toned colors. Then she stepped down into the whirring, swirling Jacuzzi.

"Ohhh, this feels wonderful," she said, letting out a long, deep sigh.

"It's better than a hot tub," said the girl.

Cassie had never been in a hot tub or a Jacuzzi. But I could really get used to this, she thought. Hooray for Hollywood!

She and the two guests introduced themselves to each other, and Cassie learned that the actors, Greg and Debra, were playing supporting roles in *Witches' Brew*.

"Have you been in many movies?" asked Cassie.

"No, this is the first time for both of us," answered Greg.

"For us *and* Rod Taggart," added Debra. "Of course, Rod's such a natural in front of a camera he seems to have been there all his life. I wonder whether he's always been this accident-prone, though."

"What have you heard?" asked Cassie innocently. She wanted to find out how much the cast knew about what was happening.

"Only that Rod has been going through a period of really bad luck," said Debra. "There've been so

55

many delays already, we're all beginning to wonder if this film will ever get made.''

So the accidents are beginning to affect everyone's morale, thought Cassie. I wonder if that's the intent.

The conversation drifted on to other subjects, and Cassie discovered that Greg and Debra had worked on tour in Ohio.

''It's nice to meet another Midwesterner who admits where she's from,'' said Debra, after they'd talked about Cassie's home state for a while. ''Some people come to Hollywood and put on an act; you know, they pretend they're used to living in all this luxury. But not me. I admit I'm impressed.''

I like her honesty, thought Cassie. I'm impressed, too.

Just then the door opened and Rod and Tanya walked in. Rod smiled at Cassie, and she felt her face heat up. She hoped Rod would think it was the effect of the hot tub.

''Hey, you guys,'' said Tanya, ''they're serving second rounds of dessert.''

''Sounds great,'' said Debra, getting up. ''Besides, I've been in here for an hour. If I don't dry off, my skin will shrivel up.'' She reached for a towel and began patting her arms and legs.

''Me too,'' Greg said, climbing out of the pool and grabbing a towel. ''How about you, Cassandra? Coming with us?''

"Thanks, but I think I'll just relax for a while," Cassie answered. She *was* relaxed, and she wanted to think over all the pieces of this puzzle.

"Okay," said Debra. "See you on the patio, Cassandra."

Debra and Greg headed for the patio with Tanya and Rod, who had waited for them. As Rod left the room, he smiled at Cassie again and said, "I'll tell Alex where you are, Cassandra. She was asking if I'd seen you."

Alone, Cassie leaned her head back against the rim of the Jacuzzi. Her eyes were closed and her legs were stretched out in front of her. She had seldom felt so light, as though she were floating on air instead of water.

Cassie drifted, allowing the events that had occurred before and since her arrival in California to play through her mind: Rod's accidents, which Alex thought couldn't be accidents; Jeff Ryan's suggestion that maybe Rod was staging his own mishaps; the threatening note Rod had received, or sent to himself; Rod's fight with Jeff, followed by Holly's words at the pool—the same words as those in Rod's note. Last of all was the one-sided conversation she'd overheard outside Marty Ingram's study.

So far, none of it added up.

The waves of the water swooshing rhythmically back and forth seemed to say, "It'll come, it'll come, it'll come. . . ."

57

Cassie let her thoughts flow with the pleasant sensation of the water. They began to lull her, in much the same way gentle waves might lure a boat from shore and cause it to drift farther and farther away. . . .

All at once Cassie felt something thrown over her head. Something rough. Terry cloth! A large towel that made it impossible for her to breathe! Someone's hand was pulling the towel tightly at the nape of her neck, while another hand was shoving her under the water!

She couldn't see, and the suffocating feeling made her kick helplessly at the water, even though she knew it was useless. Her attacker was strong and had the advantage.

Cassie's head bobbed up once, then twice, but each time it felt heavier because of the weight of the soaking-wet towel. If she didn't do something fast, she'd drown!

She tried to free her arms so she could fling the towel off and at least catch a glimpse of her assailant. But whoever it was held her left arm in a tightly locked grip; if Cassie let her right hand fall from the side of the tub, she'd have no chance!

She was doing her best not to panic, but another minute and even that wouldn't matter. Unless . . .

She could make one last attempt. A final try.

She was holding her breath as she had done immediately after the initial dunking. Luckily, her mouth hadn't been open at the moment of the surprise attack, so she hadn't breathed in any water.

But she'd been kicking and flailing her legs. Now she stopped. She let her legs and the rest of her body, including her right arm, which she dropped from the rim of the tub, go limp, as though the drowning attempt had succeeded.

As though she were dead.

For an instant, the hand that had submerged her head released its pressure.

But a moment later, it was back, shoving her farther below as if to make certain the job was finished.

Another few seconds, and it *would* be finished.

*C*assie wasn't sure why her assailant suddenly let go of her head; she only knew that one moment she was close to drowning, and the next moment she was being hauled out of the Jacuzzi. She heard what sounded like distant voices, and as they came closer she recognized one of them as Alex's.

"Cassandra! Are you all right? Speak to us! Please!"

"Maybe she needs mouth-to-mouth resuscitation." That sounded like Rod Taggart.

Slowly Cassie opened her eyes to let them know she was alive. Her eyelids still felt heavy, and her breathing was shallow and uneven. But she hadn't drowned.

"Cassandra!" cried Alex.

"Wh-what h-happened?" Cassie managed to ask between coughs and sputters.

"We found you lying on the bottom of the Jacuzzi! I thought you were joking. Then I thought you were—"

"S-somebody tried t-to drown me!" Cassie stammered as Alex helped her wrap one enormous towel around her shivering body.

"Drown you!" said Alex. "Who was it, Cassie? Do you have any idea?"

"No, he held me under the water, until—until—" Cassie was still near hysteria. Alex hugged her close.

"Cassandra, I hope you're wrong," said Rod. "Until now, all the attacks have been directed at me. You know, I did see someone sneaking out of the room that's connected to this one. . . ." Rod got up and flung open a second door. "Just as I guessed. One door leads into the hall, where I saw him, and the other leads in here. Straight to you."

Cassie's mind was still a bit foggy. She fought to clear it.

"He was wearing a long beach robe," said Rod.

"That could be any of the guests," said Cassie. She was beginning to feel better, to lose her fear.

"Well," said Rod. "He walked with a limp."

"Whoever it was had strong hands, but it could have been a man or a woman," said Cassie. Feeling dizzy, she let Rod help her into a sitting position and took over the task of toweling her hair. "I don't remember seeing anyone around here walking with a limp," she said. "What about either of you?"

Both Alex and Rod shook their heads.

"I didn't see the person at all," said Alex. "Rod's the one who noticed."

"I also noticed the robe was black velour," he offered. "Maybe that's a help."

"No," said Cassie, nodding toward the brass clothes-hook on the back of the door. Two black velour robes hung there. "I'll bet Marty leaves extra robes for his guests in every bathroom, just the way the hotel provided robes for Alex and me."

Alex checked the inside door of the bathroom connected to the Jacuzzi room, and sure enough, she returned with another black robe.

"Anyone could have slipped into one of these," Cassie said. "I think the limp may be an important clue, though."

She considered her own words, then added, "But why would someone try to drown me? Nobody but you two knows why I'm here."

"Maybe somebody suspects. Maybe he or she thinks you've found out who's behind the trouble on the set," said Alex.

"Or wants to make certain I don't."

"Cassandra," Rod interrupted, pushing back his dark hair and pacing the floor around the Jacuzzi, "I've changed my mind about your being here. I never thought it would mean so much danger for you. I want you to stay out of it from now on, okay? I can't worry about myself and you, too."

The two girls looked at each other, speechless, then stared back at Rod. "Does that mean you're going to call in the police?" Alex asked.

"I've already told you, I can take care of this myself," he protested. "You don't understand, girls— when a person is a star, they have a certain image. And my image is that of a hero. I can't afford to look like a victim! My fans wouldn't accept me that way." Rod looked genuinely worried. "This is a fickle business. Here today, gone tomorrow. At any rate, this guy's a bit of a bungler, eh? Don't you worry, I'll handle him."

Cassie was touched by Rod's honesty, and by that bit of macho pride that wouldn't let him admit his fear. "Look, Rod," she declared, "I'm in this now whether you want me or not. Someone almost drowned me. I'm not just going to overlook that."

"Maybe whoever it was planned only to scare you, Cassandra," Alex said.

"Well, he did a good job of it." Anger had come to Cassie's aid. She was now fully recovered from her misadventure, and ready to get really serious about this case. She marched past Rod. "I suggest we not mention this to anyone," she said over her shoulder.

Outside, the party was breaking up. Many of the guests were gone already. Jeff Ryan had left, too, and Rod wasn't ready to go, so Cassie and Alex rode back to the hotel with a group of actors who were also staying there.

A million questions swam around in Cassie's head. What could have tipped her assailant off to the fact that she was investigating the case? She thought she'd been as discreet as possible. Whoever had tried to drown her must have been awfully certain she posed a threat to him—or her.

And Cassie still wanted to know why Jeff and Rod had fought at the pool. Jeff hadn't answered her question earlier, and he'd made it clear that he didn't plan to.

I should have asked Rod after he and Alex pulled me out of the Jacuzzi, Cassie reflected. Of course, I did have a few other things on my mind.

Cassie and Alex practically fell into their beds. "I think a fire engine could storm through this room tonight," said Cassie, "and it wouldn't wake me. That's how tired I am."

Both girls were asleep within minutes.

Cassie awoke to the morning sun streaming through her window. The bedside clock said 7:15.

Next to it on the table was a note from Alexandra. It said: *You were sound asleep, so I went down to the restaurant to organize the notes for my story over a cup of coffee. Join me if you wake up soon. Alex.*

Cassie yawned and slipped out of bed. She pulled open the curtains and looked out the plate-glass window. In the early morning mist, Los Angeles sprawled out before her like an overgrown shopping mall. What devilish things would happen in the City of Angels today? she mused.

She went into the marble bathroom to take a long hot shower. She had just gotten dressed when she heard shouting from the hall. It sounded like Tanya Grant's voice!

"This way, Doctor!" Tanya was shouting. "Hurry, please!"

Cassie threw open the door of the suite.

"What's going on?" she called to Tanya, who was already halfway down the hall.

"It's Rod!" Tanya cried, barely stopping. "Come on, you'll see!"

Cassie ran after her. Rod's suite was down the hall and around the corner. When they entered, followed by the doctor, they saw Rod slumped in his bed, fully dressed but out cold. Beside him was a breakfast tray from room service.

Immediately, the doctor began examining the star, holding open his eyelids, feeling his pulse. Then he drew out a vial of what looked like smelling salts, and held it under Rod's nose.

With a spasm of coughing, Rod came to, rubbing his head groggily. His dark hair tumbled around his handsome face, and his skin was pale, his eyes especially dark.

"Thank goodness you're all right!" Tanya said, hugging him. "I was so frightened!"

"Just what happened before you called me, young lady?" asked the doctor, putting away his instruments as Rod slowly sat upright.

"Well, Rod didn't show up for his makeup call at six-thirty this morning," Tanya explained. "He's always on time, so at first I thought he'd overslept, and I phoned his room. There was no answer, and that's when I knew something was wrong. I got the bell captain to open Rod's door for me, and that's when we started trying to hunt you down, Doctor."

"I see," said the doctor, frowning. "The young man's going to be all right, at any rate. But to be frank with you ladies, from what I can see here, this is a matter for the police, not me."

"The police?" mumbled Rod.

"I think they should take a look at this breakfast," said the doctor.

Cassie looked again at the room-service breakfast tray. "When did this arrive?" she asked Rod.

Rod shrugged and answered groggily, "Same as every morning. I get my wakeup call at five, and breakfast is sent up at five-fifteen. Why?"

"Were you asleep when it arrived this morning?" asked Cassie.

"No, I was in the shower. Then I came out, dried off, and poured myself a cup of tea."

Cassie lifted the plate-warmer lids from the two

dishes on the tray. "You didn't touch the scrambled eggs. Or the toast."

"I didn't have a chance to," said Rod. "I sat down, drank my tea, and the next thing I remember is Tanya sitting at the edge of the bed and shaking me awake."

"Has his tea been drugged?" Cassie asked the doctor.

"Possibly," he replied. "It looks to me as though he's been given either a drug or a sedative."

"Could it be a poison, Doctor?" asked Cassie, shivering a little at the thought.

"He'd react differently to a poison," said the doctor.

Cassie had opened the metal pot that was still half filled with now-cold tea. She inhaled it, detected nothing, and handed the pot to the doctor, who also examined it.

"Whatever knocked Rod out, Doctor, wasn't put into the tea. Unless—" She interrupted herself and picked up the opened sugar packet that was lying on a saucer. She sniffed that, too, and wrinkled her nose at the smell. Then she handed the packet to the doctor.

He examined the white granules and a knowing frown crossed his face. "I think we ought to have this analyzed. But I can tell you one thing right now—this isn't sugar. It's fortunate you used only half the packet; the whole packet could have been fatal.''

On a hunch, Cassie asked, ''Rod, do you always use only half a packet of sugar in your tea?''

''Yeah,'' he answered. ''I don't like it too sweet. Never have.''

Cassie wondered how many people connected with the movie or the studio knew how much sugar he used in his tea. And whether someone hoped to kill him with the whole packet, or simply scare him with half. She also recalled Jeff Ryan's remarks about Br'er Rabbit. But would Rod actually drug himself to get publicity? Was he that desperate for attention? Cassie tried to get inside Rod's head to figure out his thinking.

His next comment seemed to point in the opposite direction.

''Look,'' he said, ''I don't want news of this to get around. I'll have a cup of strong black coffee— without sugar—and be in fine shape.''

''You're not going to shoot today,'' said Tanya.

''I certainly am,'' he said. ''And I'm serious about keeping this mum. We'll tell everyone on the set that the hotel forgot to wake me and I overslept. Okay? Please, I insist, just let me go about this in my own way.'' He shot Cassie a look that said, And you stay out of this, too—for your own good.

The doctor had put the sugar packet into a plastic envelope, which he then dropped into his black medical bag. Moving toward the door, he said, "When I hand this over to the police lab for analysis, young man, I'll have to tell them where it came from."

"If you'll give me a little time," said Rod, "I may be able to answer that without any interference from the police."

"Rod," said Tanya, "they might be of help. Think of what you may be getting yourself into."

He put an arm around her and said, "Love, I'm already into it."

"Look, young man," said the doctor, "I'll wait twenty-four hours. But that's all."

"It's a deal, Doc," said Rod. "And thanks."

When the doctor had gone, Cassie asked, "How many people know your room number, Rod?"

His answer didn't surprise her. "Everyone working on the picture. The production staff has to know where they can find me, and all the other actors from out of town are staying here at the hotel, so my room number is easy enough to find out."

"Maybe we should change your room," said Tanya in a worried voice. "Or you could move to a different hotel. That way, no one could . . ."

Rod interrupted her. "There's no need to panic," he said in a firm voice. "Besides, anyone who really wants to can always find me. There's no way I could hide for long."

The telephone rang, and Rod picked it up.

"Yeah, okay. Sorry, Marty. I'll be right there." Hanging up, he winked at Cassie. "Later, love," he said, grabbing Tanya's wrist and rushing for the door. "We've got to get to the studio. Marty's ready to kill me for being late!"

I hope Marty doesn't mean that literally, thought Cassie as Rod and Tanya raced out of the room.

*C*assie told Alex all about the tea "incident" over breakfast. By the time the two girls had returned to their room, Tanya Grant was calling from the studio.

"We've rescheduled the witches' coven bit for this afternoon instead of tomorrow," said Tanya in a businesslike voice. "It's a crowd scene, and I wondered if you and Alex might like to be in it," she told Cassie.

Cassie's eyes widened. A chance to do some undercover investigating *and* be in the film at the same time! I'll be there and I'll do my "best," she thought.

Cassie took a deep breath and answered, "Why, yes, Tanya, we'd love to. But how can we be in the film if we're not members of Screen Actors Guild?"

"No problem," Tanya assured her. "Usually you'd need a SEG card. That's Screen Extras Guild. But this is such a big crowd scene, we're allowed to use some non-union extras. How about it?"

Alex, who had come closer to the phone while

brushing her hair, nodded eagerly as Cassie said, "Just tell us when and where."

Tanya gave them directions and an appointment for their costume fittings at Wardrobe B. "I have a zillion calls to make," she said, "so I'll see you both later on the set."

"Okay," agreed Cassie, hanging up the phone and, despite the real reason for her being in Hollywood, feeling that she was about to begin the most exciting day of her life.

"We have only an hour," teased Alex as Cassie sat down in front of the mirror and began reapplying her makeup.

"That'll give us just about enough time. We don't want to look washed-out under the lights."

"Oh, right," said Alex, seating herself beside Cassie and starting to add highlight here and shadow there to emphasize the contours of her peaches-and-cream complexion.

Suddenly an idea struck Cassie. "Alex!" she exclaimed. "I've just had a brainstorm. Let's telephone Peter Wentworth in London!" Peter was a handsome young newspaperman whom Cassie had met during her visit to England.

"Well, Cassandra, aside from your having taken a fancy to him, and vice-versa, have you a specific reason for ringing him, or is it simply to tell him we're going to be in a movie?"

"No, it's for information. After all, he is an investigative reporter on your father's paper. He has access to files and could help us by gathering some facts.''

''Facts? Such as . . . ?''

''Such as the facts behind the rumors about Rod Taggart and Holly Chiswick, and why they broke up.'' Cassie felt the more she knew about Rod, the better. If he was, indeed, causing all these problems himself, maybe there was something in his background that would tip her off to his motives.

''What do you hope to learn from that?'' asked Alex.

Cassie shrugged. ''I'm not sure. But there may be something, either from the time the British Bombshell lived in London, or going further back to Rod's early years in Liverpool. It might add some pieces to the puzzle.''

''Good idea,'' said Alex. ''Anything I can do?''

''Well, I don't have Peter's telephone number with me.''

Alex went to her purse and pulled out a thick address book. ''The only number I have is his office extension at the newspaper.'' She looked at her watch. ''If you ring him right now, you may still catch him before he leaves for the evening. It's going on dinner at home.''

Alex gave Cassie the long list of numbers to dial for the international operator and, while Cassie waited for Peter to answer, Alex added a third coat of mascara to her upper lashes, this time in vivid purple.

"Cassandra!" Peter Wentworth's voice was clearer than that of the hotel switchboard downstairs. "How marvelous to hear your voice!"

"Same here, Peter!" Cassie could hardly believe she was talking to him.

Cassie glanced across the room at her friend, who crossed her heart melodramatically and whispered, "Romeo, Romeo, wherefore art thou, Romeo?"

Cassie made a silly face and turned back to the phone. After catching up on a bit of personal news, Cassie told Peter about the trouble on the set and finished by saying, "So Alex and I thought you might be able to help. I need information. Anything you can find out about Rod Taggart and his ex-girlfriend, Holly Chiswick.

"Whatever I can dig up," Peter said. "But tell me, are they under suspicion of some crime?"

"Not exactly. Why do you say that?"

"Oh, no reason in particular," he answered. "I just seem to recall rumors of a scandal. But I suppose that's what you want, isn't it? To find out whether there's any truth to the stories?"

"Yes. Whatever you can find out about his background, his friends, his enemies. We'll be on the set

74

all day, but the sooner you can let us know the better."

"Let me have the studio's number," said Peter. "I'll ring you there later, or at your hotel around midnight, your time."

"All right," Cassie said. "But if you have to call me at the studio, be careful what you say, just in case someone is listening in on an extension phone."

"Right-o," he said. "I'll get on it ASAP."

"Thanks, Peter," said Cassie. "What you come up with may help us solve the case."

After Cassie hung up, she and Alex drove to Wardrobe B. The building was so big, it was more like a warehouse.

Cassie had tried to imagine what kinds of costumes she and Alex would be given to wear. In the car, they described the fabulous gowns from some of their favorite movies.

However, what awaited the girls when they entered Wardrobe B were rows and rows of some of the ugliest costumes Cassie had ever seen.

"Are they serious?" she asked, gazing up at hundreds, maybe thousands, of dull, drab cloaks, robes, and capes.

She touched the rough burlap of one particularly disgusting-looking costume that looked and smelled as if it had spent years in a damp cave.

"You don't think we're in the wrong place, do you?" asked Alex.

Just then, the door to Wardrobe B opened and a chubby, smiling woman said, "Oh, are you extras for *Witches' Brew?*"

Cassie turned to Alex and frowned. "Unfortunately, I think we're in the right place." To the wardrobe woman, she said, "Yes, Tanya Grant told us to come here."

The woman eyed both girls, then went to the rack on the farthest wall. "Well, then, take your pick from those. They'll all be about the right length."

"You mean we needn't be fitted, or anything like that?" asked Alex.

The woman shook her head. "Nope. There'll be so many of you in the scene, if every one of you had to be measured, we'd be here till Christmas. Besides, you'll all be huddled together in the background while the 'devil' sings his chant. Most of the work will be for the special-effects guys with their cauldron and dry-ice stuff."

Alex sighed. "We'd have looked better in those beach robes at Marty Ingram's house."

Cassie narrowed her eyes and said, "Considering that someone wearing one of them tried to drown me, Alex, I'll pretend you didn't say that."

They headed for the extras' dressing room, where they could slip out of their clothes before putting on the long, heavy robes. As they passed by the studio message board, Cassie's eyes skimmed it idly. She stopped short when she saw a folded note tacked to the board. It read: TAGGART.

"Just a moment, Alex," she said. "I think the anonymous writer has struck again." She indicated the typed note. "I don't usually open other people's mail, but as a good detective I think I ought to make an exception. What do you think?"

Alex nodded her agreement as Cassie took down the note and unfolded it.

"Sure enough, it's from the same person," Cassie said. "Listen to this." She read aloud:

> *Roses are red,*
> *Violets are blue,*
> *Sugar is sweet,*
> *And deadly too.*
>
> *There is more trouble brewing*
> *in your future.*

"Rod will be furious when he reads that," Alex said when Cassie had finished. "Do you think we ought to leave it for him?"

"He'd be even more furious if he found out we were interfering," Cassie answered. "Maybe this will convince him he needs our help."

"Maybe," said Alex dubiously as Cassie retacked the note to the board. "Or maybe he'll just decide to play hero for real."

Well, thought Cassie later as she and Alex milled around Soundstage A in their monklike robes, soon we'll be on an honest-to-goodness movie set! And Tanya did mention that some of the extras may be given a line or two of dialogue!

Cassie saw more and more extras arriving. They were all dressed in similar burlap robes tied with twine.

"Okay, background people! Over here!" The girls were leaning against a wall off to the side when the assistant yelled the order. He repeated it, but Cassie and Alex didn't pay attention until he came over to them and said, "Ladies, if you please. Background people means you, too. You *are* extras in this scene, aren't you?"

Embarrassed, Cassie said, "Yes. Background people. Sorry."

He motioned them down a hall. "Well, you can't miss the set, girls. It looks like an underground cave. Now, shall we?" Cassie and Alex joined the mob of other robed extras heading for the cave set she'd seen the first day. So far, she mused, work as a movie extra is less than thrilling.

Two hours had passed, and by now Marty had called "Action!" and "Cut!" so many times that Cassie had lost count. Stop and start, stop and start. She felt a little dazed from watching take after take of the same scene. The extras were moving like zombies, and even Jeff Ryan seemed subdued. He sat quietly by the camera, flicking cigar ashes onto the floor, looking too bored to pun.

The assistant director had herded Cassie and Alex and a dozen or more extras into one part of the set that dripped with stalactites and stalagmites made of painted Styrofoam. Their "part" was simply to say "Yes!" whenever the assistant, from the sidelines, nodded his head up and down, and to cry "No!" when he shook his head from side to side.

"Some acting!" whispered Cassie under her breath.

"You there!" called the assistant director, pointing to Cassie.

Uh-oh, she thought. This is like school, and the teacher has just caught me talking in class!

She couldn't hide anywhere; except for Alex, Cassie was taller than any of the extras in their group.

The assistant came up to her, and Cassie was certain she was what one extra had called "dead on the picture." Her only role in the movies was about to be terminated.

"You're Cassandra Best, right?" he said.

"Yes, I am."

"Listen, you're not needed in the next shot, and there's a phone call for you. Transatlantic, so I figured it might be important. You can take it in Marty's office."

Peter! "Oh, yes, thank you!"

The assistant showed her the way, and soon she heard Peter's voice exclaim, "Cassandra! I have news. Is it safe to talk?"

"It's fine," she said. "Everyone's on the set. What did you find?"

"Well, a few things. First of all, Rod ran around with a pretty wild group before he became a star. It was more of an old-fashioned street gang, actually. You know, fighting with other gangs over territory, that sort of thing. In fact, Rod's been something of a brawler throughout his career, and especially during his breakup with the British Bombshell. It's been, 'Photographers and inquisitive reporters beware,' if you get my meaning."

Cassie did. "Brawlers make a lot of enemies, don't they?" she said.

"Usually, that's true," Peter agreed. "But aside from a few angry newspeople, Rod doesn't seem to have stepped on too many toes on his way to the top. Apparently, he's a nice guy for all his toughness. I can't find evidence of bad blood between him and anyone else at all."

"So he doesn't have *any* enemies?" said Cassie. "Okay, what else?"

"Well, he was a very big spender over here. It could be simply because he was so poor when he was a kid and the sudden stardom went to his head."

"Peter," said Cassie, "what are you hinting at?"

"All right, here it is. Mr. Rodney Allen Taggart

has spent every shilling he ever earned in England. And he's still in debt. Furthermore, Rod took out a huge insurance policy just before he left for the States to star in *Witches' Brew*."

"Well, he was traveling to a foreign country," Cassie said, trying to remain objective.

"Cassandra, it's not that kind of insurance policy."

"What do you mean?"

"Merely this. He's insured himself against failure to complete the film. If anything happens so *Witches' Brew* can't finish shooting, Rod will receive almost twice the money he's being paid for starring in the film!"

Cassie's head was swirling. "Peter, you're saying he'll wind up richer if he *doesn't* make the movie?"

"Exactly. Which ties in with the possibility that he may need the insurance money to pay off his creditors."

"So," Cassie answered slowly, "Jeff Ryan may have been right about Br'er Rabbit."

"I don't understand," said Peter.

"It's just that Rod may be staging these accidents himself."

Cassie's mind flashed back to the Jacuzzi attack. Rod couldn't have been responsible for that. Surely he wouldn't try to kill her. But who else besides Rod knew Cassie was a detective? "Anyway, I hope I'm wrong," she said to Peter.

She looked at her wristwatch and saw that she'd been away from the set for more than ten minutes.

"Peter, I'd better go. I can't thank you enough for your help."

"Well, I hope it leads to a solution. Keep me posted. And Cassandra, there's one more thing." His voice had taken on a strange tone.

"Yes, Peter?"

"Be careful. Private investigating can be a deadly business."

"Yes, Peter, I know."

"If Rod Taggart is desperate enough to hurt himself just to get the shoot closed down, there's no telling who else he might hurt."

*C*assie made her way back to the set, where Marty was still shooting the same scene that was being set up when Peter's call had come through.

She walked over to the group of extras to which she and Alex had been assigned.

"Anything important?" whispered Alex.

"You bet!" said Cassie.

She was about to go into more detail when the clapper called, "*Witches' Brew*, scene seventeen, take six." He clapped the chalkboard while the camera photographed it up close, then he crept quickly out of range and the actors moved in.

Cassie knew that in this scene the rock star was going to fight the leader of the coven before rescuing his girlfriend. She was curious to see how Rod looked in action.

This take wasn't a close-up, so at first Cassie thought she was watching Rod, as the tall, lanky actor strode onto the scene and landed a surprise punch in the stomach of the movie's "devil."

The fight had been carefully staged, Cassie knew, so that no one would get hurt. It seemed impossible not to get hurt, though, the way both men kept falling back against the craggy-looking stones. But Cassie remembered the stones were made of Styrofoam. She relaxed and began to enjoy the fight, which more and more took on the feeling of a choreographed ballet.

At the end of the scene, she heard Marty yell, "Cut!" and Cassie realized the tall actor was Sky Bowman dressed as Rod Taggart. The stuntman went limping off the set.

Limping! Cassie's heart skipped a beat. "Alex!" she whispered frantically. "Did you notice that? Sky Bowman is limping!"

Alex's eyes widened. "Cassandra, you're right!"

"Was he limping in the five earlier takes while I was gone?" asked Cassie.

"I can't say for certain. But if he was—"

"If he was, he just might be the same person who was limping at Marty's party after he nearly drowned me!"

"Quiet!" came the assistant's voice. "We're going for one more take and then we'll set up for the gunshot sequence."

The clapper went through his routine and take seven began to roll.

Cassie watched the fight once more and this time studied Sky Bowman to see if he favored his right foot. Sure enough, he did.

Her mind darted back to Marty's house and the Jacuzzi. Had Sky Bowman been limping at the party? She couldn't remember.

A moment later, Marty called, "Cut! Hey, Sky, what's the matter with your ankle all of a sudden?"

"Sorry, Marty," Sky replied. "I must have twisted it during that last take."

"All right, everybody!" Marty said. Then he whispered something to his assistant, who called, "Okay, people, a ten-minute break and then we go again. Rita, let's get an Ace bandage over here and tape up his ankle. On the double!"

The woman named Rita raced off to a corner and was back a moment later with a first-aid kit.

"Well, that shoots your theory, doesn't it?" said Alex. Then she apologized. "Oops, I'm frightfully sorry about that. Jeff Ryan's puns really do rub off!"

Smiling in spite of herself, Cassie nodded. "You're right on both counts. Sky's in the clear, unless his ankle was hurt before and he just didn't let on. Maybe the fight scene only made it worse."

Then she tossed out that idea. Someone with a sprained ankle wouldn't be able to do those fight scenes in the first place. And Sky's ankle would already have been taped. From where the girls stood, Cassie could see that there wasn't any tape under the bandage Rita was rolling around the stuntman's ankle.

"Okay, back to square one," Cassie said aloud. "Which leaves us where we were, except for the information Peter's been able to give me."

"Tell me everything!" said Alex. "Before they start shooting again!"

"Okay," answered Cassie. "But you're not going to like it much." She filled Alex in on Peter's findings as well as his suspicions.

When she had finished, Alex said quietly, "Cassandra, I simply cannot believe, not even for a minute, that Rod Taggart is involved in an insurance scam."

"I hope you're right, Alex. But now it's more important than ever to find out the truth and prove it, one way or the other."

Alex started to say something, but Rita had finished taping Sky Bowman's ankle, and Marty Ingram was ready to go again.

"Action!" yelled the assistant. The clapper reappeared and shooting of take eight followed.

More than half the extras were dismissed before the dinner break, but Tanya Grant had come by a few moments earlier and had said to Cassie and Alex, "Both of you are in the scenes we're shooting tonight, so please don't wander too far from the set."

Because Marty was planning to continue shooting into the evening, everyone was served a boxed dinner. This way, the actors and extras wouldn't have to leave the set for a meal at the studio commissary.

When they'd finished eating, the girls still had a few minutes left before the end of the break, so they took a leisurely stroll around the set. Cassie noticed Rod standing where they'd been shooting all afternoon. If the note on the bulletin board had angered him, he didn't show it. All his attention was concentrated on rehearsing a fall, as though he'd just been shot.

Alex and Cassie watched from the sidelines. A voice called, "Bang!" Then Rod's arms and legs seemed to fold in, and his body looked as if it had collapsed on itself.

"That's better, but it still looks staged," said the voice from behind one of the cave's Styrofoam boulders.

"Yeah, well, I did it the way you told me to, Sky," said Rod. "You've had more experience, so it looks real when you do it."

"Well, let me show you again." Sky Bowman came out to join Rod, and from where the girls stood, the actor and his stunt-double could have passed for twins.

"It's amazing!" whispered Alex. "Two tall, gorgeous men."

"It sure is!" agreed Cassie. "I know all the famous stars use doubles for dangerous stunts, but when you see them side by side, it looks like trick photography!"

She grew quiet as the two actors began another rehearsal.

"Okay," said Sky, "you say it, and I'll do the falling this time."

"Right," answered Rod. He raised his right hand and pointed his index finger as if it were a pistol. "Bang!" he yelled.

Sky Bowman doubled over into a heap. Cassie almost cried out when she saw him fall to the floor.

"There! You see the difference?" asked Sky, getting up and brushing himself off. "Your whole body has to contract, almost into a ball."

Rod nodded. "I think I get it now. Let's take five and we'll try it one last time. I just want to get a can of soda." Sky limped over to Rod, and together they walked off in the direction of the vending machines.

"That looked so real!" exclaimed Alex. "I mean, if I'd heard an actual gun blast, I'd swear that he'd been shot!"

"Movies really are a matter of illusion," mused Cassie aloud.

"What?"

"I read that somewhere in a book about the history of motion pictures. It said that things on film aren't what our eyes are actually seeing, but instead are what the directors and technicians and special-effects people make us *believe* we're seeing. Illusions. Even Jeff Ryan pointed that out.''

''I was under the impression this afternoon, with all our sitting around and waiting, that you were somewhat disappointed in the art of moviemaking,'' remarked Alex.

''Only with the slowness of the way a film is shot,'' answered Cassie. ''And the constant repeating of the same scene, over and over again. But I'm still amazed by the results.''

She was so lost in thought, she didn't notice the red light flashing over the exit door. She did hear the three bells, though, and knew that meant Marty had resumed shooting. No extras were needed in this sequence. It was the scene the girls had seen Rod and Sky rehearsing. Cassie and Alex huddled just out of camera range and watched, along with another forty or fifty extras who hadn't been dismissed for the day.

The star stood with his back to the girls and to the cameras. There was a loud *Bang!* and he dropped. But not the way Sky had taught Rod to curl up and collapse into a ball. Instead, his arms went out in a wide-open position, as though he'd been shot in the back.

He fell, not into a heap, but against the table, and both went down.

''Cut!'' yelled Marty, rushing forward from his chair beside the cameraman. ''Rod, what in heaven's name—'' He stopped short when he reached the overturned table and the slumped-over actor.

''It's not Rod!'' Marty cried, shaking his head in bewilderment. ''It's *Sky!* He's been shot for real!''

The hum of anxious voices filled the soundstage as cast and crew reacted in shock. Above the din, Marty's assistant shouted, ''Get an ambulance!''

While Rita rushed forward to offer assistance, Cassie turned to Alex and said, ''I thought Rod was going to do his own stunt. Isn't that why he was rehearsing earlier with Sky?''

''It's certainly the way things looked,'' said Alex. Then softly, she added, ''But that's what you've been saying all along, isn't it, Cassandra? About movies being a matter of illusion?''

As the two girls, along with the other people who had seen the shooting, hurried closer, Cassie noticed one of the hooded, robed extras moving farther and farther away from the center of activity—and the person was limping!

''Alex!'' she whispered. ''Stay here and find out what you can. I'll be back.''

''Be careful!'' Alex replied. ''Sky wasn't shot with a blank.''

Cassie quickly edged her way through the crowd, while trying to keep an eye on the person heading for the exit door.

But was he or she the would-be killer? she wondered, following the robe but afraid to call out

"Stop!" in case the person was still carrying a loaded pistol.

"Coming through!" yelled a paramedic at the front end of a stretcher. Cassie jumped out of the way, and in so doing, she lost sight of the fleeing culprit.

She hurried down the hall to the exit door, where she found a security guard sitting at his post.

"Did you see someone wearing a brown robe with a hood go dashing out of here a minute ago?" she asked.

"Sure did. Thought the place must be on fire. Why?"

"Was it a man or a woman?"

The guard took off his cap and scratched his head. "Don't know, miss. It happened so fast. And right on the heels of the emergency guys, too. What's going on, anyway?"

"There's been an accident on the set," Cassie explained, not bothering with details. "Listen, can you tell if the person walked with a limp?"

"*Ran* with one is more like it, miss. Bolted out of here quicker than lightning."

"Did you notice anything that you might recognize if you saw the person again?"

"How could I, miss?" asked the guard. "The way everybody's dressed around here today, why, you all look alike."

Cassie checked the area outside the soundstage,

but she saw no one wearing a robe. Some detective she was. She'd witnessed a shooting, followed a suspect, actually had him in sight, then lost him. Great. And with her luck, the person probably wasn't even working as an extra at all.

She made her way back to the set and walked over to Rod, Tanya, and Alex. They were seated in canvas chairs away from the center of activity and talking in low voices. Sky Bowman was being taken to the hospital, and Alex whispered that the police were on their way.

"I feel as if it's my fault," said Rod. "And this time, there'll be no way to keep it out of the papers."

Tanya tried to help. "Maybe Marty and Jeff can get them to keep it quiet for now. But whatever happens, Rod, you mustn't blame yourself. You had no way of knowing—"

"But don't you see?" he interrupted. "*I* was supposed to do the stunt, not Sky!"

"Then why did he wind up doing it?" asked Cassie. "Alex and I saw you and Sky rehearsing, and it didn't seem like a difficult stunt."

"Sky insisted," said Rod. "I *was* going to do the stunt, but at the last minute, he told me he thought it looked phony when I fell. If I'd learned to fall the way Sky was trying to teach me"—his face went pale—"I'd have been shot instead of Sky." In a whisper, he added, "The bullet was meant for me. I owe Sky my life."

For the first time, Cassie sensed that Rod was truly frightened. Maybe he wasn't trying to sabotage his own picture, after all.

Still, he could have *not* mastered his fall on purpose, so Sky would insist on doing the stunt. But that would mean Rod was working with a partner, because Rod had been on the set the whole time.

Or had he?

Cassie thought back to the stunt. No, Rod hadn't been on the set. Of course, she reasoned, he wasn't the person I chased, either. Whoever that was got out of the building. No one on the set now could have been the robed suspect.

Cassie scanned the crowd. "Alex, did Holly go to the hospital with Sky?"

"I don't think so," Alex replied.

Cassie realized she hadn't seen Holly since dinner.

Rod and Tanya got up from their chairs. "I'll drive us back to the hotel," said Tanya. "I don't know yet what Marty plans to do, but he's wrapped for tonight, and I for one don't want to stick around here."

"That's two of us," said Rod. Cassie saw that despite his smile, his hands were shaking.

"Get some sleep," she advised.

"Yeah, right," he said. Then he added sarcastically, "I'll just add extra sugar to my tea."

*T*he following morning the atmosphere on the set of *Witches' Brew* was quiet. Even the electricians and carpenters went about their business making as little noise as possible. Sky Bowman had undergone surgery to remove the bullet, and he'd been lucky; no vital organs had been hit. But his condition was still listed as serious, and while nobody talked much about it, everyone waited anxiously for the latest medical report.

The police had questioned every actor, extra, crew member, and employee who had been in or around the area of Soundstage A the evening before. Cassie learned from Tanya Grant that the police had talked with Marty Ingram and Jeff Ryan, and had agreed to keep the investigation as quiet as they could for now.

''The police captain said that might not be easy, though,'' explained Tanya, ''because a film starring Rod Taggart is news. And an accident that threatens a star's life is *big* news. That's what Rod's been afraid of all along,'' she finished.

"I always thought movie stars wanted as much publicity as they could get," said Cassie.

"Not Rod," returned Tanya. "It's one of the interesting things about him. He's a very private person. Sure, he likes being in the limelight, but only *on* the set, not off it. He'd hate it if news about the shooting leaked to the press."

"You seem to know quite a bit about him," said Cassie.

"I know what Rod is like," Tanya said, "but that's from spending so much time with him. I just know he's the warmest, most honest and loyal person I've ever met."

Marty called to her then, and Tanya said, "You'll have to excuse me. The show must go on."

She's very fond of Rod, thought Cassie. I wonder if she's protecting him.

After Tanya had gone, Cassie headed back toward Rod's dressing room. She needed to ask him so many things—about his fight with Jeff Ryan and his relationship with Holly Chiswick. Cassie was convinced that one way or another, Rod Taggart held the key to this mystery.

She found him at the message board outside his dressing room. He was intently studying a note that he had pulled off the board. When he saw Cassie, he tried to hide the note behind his back.

"Oh! Hello there!" he said, a little too cheerfully. "I heard the report that Sky's holding his own."

"Yes," Cassie said. "How about you?"

"Me? Oh, fine, just fine," he said nervously.

"What's that note behind your back?" said Cassie, taking the direct approach.

Rod hesitated. "I told you, Cassandra, I want to handle this business myself from now on. It's too dangerous for you to get any more involved with."

"And I told you," she replied coolly, "I'm not getting off the case. Whoever is causing the trouble here tried to kill me, too, remember? The note," she repeated, putting out her hand. For the moment, Cassie had totally forgotten she was speaking with the superfamous Rod Taggart. Right now, she was just doing her "best" to solve this case.

Rod sighed and handed her the note. "Right," he said. "It's another threat, as you can see. In fact, it's my third," he added grimly. The note read:

Practice makes perfect.
Next time there'll be
no mistakes.
Ta-ta, Falling Star.

It had obviously been typed on the same kind of paper as the first two notes and it had the same typeface.

"Well," said Rod, when Cassie had finished reading. "What do you think?"

"Just what I thought about the first note," she

replied. "This person is very dangerous. What did the second note say?" she asked, as if she hadn't read it.

Rod recited the "Roses are red" poem by heart. "But this is the last threat ever," he continued. "I'm going to find out who this person is, pronto. And when I do," he added, his face grim, "I'm going to take care of the problem. My way."

So saying, Rod turned and walked off in the direction of the exit door.

Cassie read the new note again as she wandered back to the set where Sky had been shot. When she got there, she saw two people seated on benches that had been covered to look like boulders. Jeff Ryan was leaning forward and talking in a low voice to Holly Chiswick as Cassie joined them.

"Good morning," said Jeff. "Any news about Sky?"

At the mention of his name, Holly burst into tears. Her eyes were already red from crying.

Cassie shook her head.

"Well, can't anyone do anything?" asked Holly. "If the police had been involved from the start, Sky wouldn't be—" She was too choked up to finish the sentence.

"Hey, c'mon, cheer up, Holly," said Jeff, taking one of his ever-present cigars from a pocket. He removed the cellophane and the paper cigar ring, then slid the ring onto Holly's middle finger. It made her smile; the ring was double her finger's size.

Jeff reached into another pocket. This time he came up empty. "Anybody got a match? I'm fresh out."

Holly reached into her shoulder bag and said, "Here, Jeff. But let me have it back." She handed the producer a silver matchbook.

He lifted the cover and pulled out a match. But before striking it, he studied the embossed cowboy boot on the cover. "Hey, this is unusual, Holly."

"May I see it?" Cassie asked casually. Jeff handed the matchbook to her.

It's the same as the matchbook I found at Marty Ingram's party! thought Cassie. "The Silver Spur in Las Vegas," she said, reading the name of the casino aloud and pretending she'd never seen it before.

"Oh, yes!" said Holly. She smiled, then suddenly seemed on the verge of tears. "It's—it's a souvenir of the first time I met Sky. I was working for Marty on *Gambler's Gold* in Las Vegas. Maybe you remember the picture?" she asked Cassie hopefully.

"Yes, I do," said Cassie. She remembered it all right. It had been an awful picture, and Holly Chiswick had been awful in it.

"Well," Holly went on, cheered by the fact that Cassie had seen the picture, "one night in the casino, Marty introduced me to Sky. We started talking, waiting for Marty to finish at the blackjack table.'' Holly gave a little laugh. ''Marty was playing the game for hours, so Sky and I had lots of time to get acquainted.''

''I didn't know Marty was into blackjack,'' said Cassie.

''Oh, yes.'' Holly laughed. ''He's a real high roller. And he was on a big roll that night. Sky and I finally gave up and left without him. We've been together ever since—''

Holly stopped, the tears coming again. Holding her hand out for the matchbook, she whispered, ''And I've kept that ever since, too.''

''It makes a nice souvenir,'' said Cassie gently, handing the matchbook back to Holly just as Tanya and Alex arrived.

Tanya's face wore a serious expression, and Cassie guessed that she'd been on the phone with the hospital.

She was right.

''I have an update on Sky,'' said Tanya. ''And it's not very good.''

Holly's eyes flooded once more with tears. ''Oh no. Is he . . . is he . . . ?''

''He's back in surgery. But the doctor said not to lose hope.''

''Ohhhh!'' Holly's entire body had begun to tremble as her hands flew to her face and sobs gushed forth. Alex ran to find Rita, and soon the

studio nurse was leading the hysterical Holly Chiswick away.

The girls left Jeff Ryan and Tanya Grant sitting
together on the bench.

"Did you see that?" Cassie asked Alex when they
were alone outside on the lot.

"See what? Holly's reaction?"

"No, the way she was walking. Limping, that is.
And it wasn't because she was leaning on Rita."

"I thought I'd imagined it," said Alex.

"Not for a minute," said Cassie.

Marty Ingram had decided not to resume shooting
until that afternoon. He'd called a meeting in his
office with Jeff Ryan and the rest of the production
staff. It was just breaking up when Cassie and Alex
returned from a meeting of their own, during which
they'd made a list of the clues they'd found so far.

Now, as several people filed out of the office
and headed down different hallways, Cassie and
Alex wandered along the corridor that housed the
executive offices. The girls were passing Marty Ingram's door when they heard two people arguing
loudly.

Grabbing Alex's arm, Cassie stopped and leaned
closer.

"Look, Jeff," Marty was saying. "I want to end it
now. This can't go on!"

"You made a deal, Marty," countered Jeff. "You can't back out. We're in this together."

Are they talking about the picture? wondered Cassie.

"Jeff, I'm the director, and I'm calling the shots!"

"That sounds like one of my puns, Marty," Jeff said with a laugh.

"This is no joke, Jeff. I don't think so, and neither do the police."

"You'll have to keep them out of this, Marty. For all our sakes." Jeff paused, then said, "We'll talk later. Right now I've got some other business to take care of." His voice grew louder.

"Pssssst," hissed Cassie. "He's coming toward the door. We'd better get out of here. Fast!"

Together Cassie and Alex raced from the building.

"What do you think that was all about?" asked Alex, when they stopped to catch their breath.

"I don't know, but I have some theories. Marty said, 'I want to end it now.' "

"End what?" asked Alex.

"Maybe the shooting," answered Cassie. "But the conversation I overheard at his house suggested that he needs money. So that just doesn't add up." Cassie twisted her hair up off her neck. Outside it was hot and humid. She leaned on the wall by the soundstage door, mulling over some of the facts she'd put together.

Try as she might, she couldn't make herself believe that Rod wanted this picture to fail. Maybe someone really was trying to kill Rod. But *who?*

Or maybe *someone else* wanted the picture to fail!

Cassie turned to Alex. "Remember Peter said that Rod had taken out a large insurance policy that would pay off if this picture folded? I wonder if the production company could have a similar policy. If so, we might be able to discover someone besides Rod who'd profit if the picture closed down."

"You may be onto something, Cassandra Best," Alex said, jerking open the soundstage door. The girls walked toward the set, where a crew was setting lights for the afternoon's shooting.

"I'm going to give Peter a call," said Cassie. "With his connections as a reporter, he should be able to dig around and find out what kind of insurance the picture has. Then I'm going to find a quiet spot and rethink a few things."

"Well, don't think too long," Alex said. "Shooting starts at two o'clock, remember? See you later, Cassandra. I'm famished. Can I bring you something from the commissary?"

"No thanks," Cassie said with a smile. "I'm not very hungry."

Alex laughed. "Oh, Cassandra Best, you're never hungry when the wheels are spinning in that brain of yours. All the same, I'm going to bring you something to eat. See you later."

After Alex left, Cassie found a phone and dialed Peter in London.

"I'll get back to you, Cassandra," said Peter when she'd told him what she needed. "This case is becoming really fascinating, isn't it? But Cassandra—you are taking care of yourself, aren't you?"

"I certainly am," said Cassie, nervously glancing around to make sure no one was nearby.

"Good. We wouldn't want anything to happen to you," said Peter. "Cheerio, for now."

"Bye." Hanging up, Cassie took a deep breath and blew it out again. She felt restless and decided to go outside for a walk, hot and humid though it was. She needed to clear her head and think things through.

Then, out of the corner of her eye, Cassie detected a sudden movement. She spun around, but no one was there. Funny . . . she'd had the same feeling while she was on the phone with Peter.

Oh well, I'm probably just being paranoid, she thought.

Just to make sure she wasn't being followed, she decided to double back to where she'd seen the movement. There was no one around. Cassie continued in the same direction, uncertain whether she heard footsteps far behind her. Every time she stopped, so did the footsteps. An echo? she wondered.

She walked outside, crossing the lot aimlessly,

every now and then looking behind her to see if she was being followed. Nothing.

She was now standing outside an old warehouse. It was the building Sky had shown her that first day, the one with all the animal costumes. Smiling as she remembered, Cassie pushed open the unlocked door marked Wardrobe D and stepped inside.

It was cool in there. Apparently, the studio kept it air-conditioned to preserve the costumes. Cassie wandered down the hallway to the door of the room where she thought the animals were stored. Curious to look at them again, Cassie was about to push the door open, when she heard familiar voices inside. Rod and Tanya were talking, and from the sound of it, it was an intense discussion.

"Rod, I'm begging you for your own good," Tanya was saying.

"Tanya, I know what I'm doing. You've got to trust me."

"I do trust you. I just don't want you to get killed!" She sounded near tears.

"I'll be all right. That's a promise, too."

Cassie's hand on the doorknob slipped, and the door rattled. Cassie could hear Tanya's frantic whisper, then the sound of running footsteps.

Cassie threw open the door and ran inside, just in time to hear a door slam at the other end of the wardrobe room.

Rats! Cassie had blown a perfect eavesdropping

opportunity! Now she might never find out what Tanya and Rod were doing here, and what they were being so secretive about.

Alone, Cassie looked around the wardrobe room. Aside from thousands of costumes, there was nothing to see. Tired, Cassie sat down on a trunk and thought, trying to put herself inside the minds of the different suspects:

Holly Chiswick. She's developed a limp, and she seems too upset about everything. Had she tried to get rid of Rod to make Sky a star?

Jeff Ryan. Those puns of his are enough to send him to jail for poor taste. Was someone trying to make it look as if Jeff had written those threatening notes to Rod? And just what did Jeff and Rod fight about at the party?

Marty Ingram. During the party at his house someone tried to kill me—after I overheard his phone conversation. But he couldn't have seen me. What about his argument with Jeff this morning? Is it linked to Sky's shooting?

Tanya Grant. She seems ready to do anything to protect Rod Taggart. But would she cover up for him?

And of course, Rod himself. I still can't rule him out, either.

Cassie was thinking so intently that she didn't hear the sound behind her.

It was the creepy feeling up the back of her spine that made her spin around.

When she did, it was too late. She was staring into the weird, grinning face of a gorilla!

Then something covered her mouth, and everything went black.

Chapter 10

*C*assie opened her eyes to almost total darkness. At first she thought she'd been here, wherever "here" was, for hours, and that the sun had already set. Then, little by little, she became aware of her surroundings.

The odor of mothballs filled her nostrils, and as her eyes adjusted to the darkness, the shadows became outlines of huge jungle animals. Lions and bears and . . . gorillas.

But before she could dwell on the gorilla that was her last memory, she smelled another odor. Smoke! And the suffocating smell was growing stronger. It was coming from inside the warehouse!

She tried to get up, but her arms and legs were tied in front of her. Who had done this? The "gorilla"?

She started to cough. Her ribs ached as she inhaled slowly and exhaled deeply. At least she was on the floor, the safest place to be in the middle of a fire. No, the safest place was outside. She must get out!

Bringing her hands up to her face, she rubbed her wrists gently against her cheek. The knots were of a furry-feeling fabric. Animal tails! The idea seemed almost funny to Cassie. So she was tied up with the tails of animal costumes. She felt just as trapped as if it were solid rope. But maybe not. She put her teeth to work on the knots.

The smoke got thicker, smelling now of acrid burning latex and rubber. Her eyes began to burn and water from the irritation. Leaning her head between her legs, she tried to breathe what little air was left low on the floor. If she blacked out because of inhaling the smoke, she would be dead. Dead—the word spurred her on.

"Heeeelp," she screamed as loudly as possible. "Help! Fire! Please someone help me!"

Nothing.

The crackling of the flames and the thick layers of animal costuming absorbed all her cries. No one would hear her. She was on her own. Perhaps no one had even discovered the fire yet.

Acting is believing. She remembered Gran's words of advice. Gran—her family—would she ever see them again? She must stay calm enough to save herself. Acting is believing. She must act as if it were possible. Stay calm and take one step at a time.

Cassie began to bite on the huge, taut knot at her wrist. Bits of furry fabric kept coming off in her mouth. She spat them out, then chewed and tugged again. Still, the knot refused to come undone.

Then, thinking furiously, Cassie came up with another idea. The knots were tied tightly above her wide wristwatch strap. If she couldn't bite through the fabric ties, maybe she could undo the buckle of her watch strap. With her wrist free of the watch, she might be able to slide her hand through the tie.

Carefully she brought the leather strap to her mouth. She coughed, breathed what little clear air remained, then took the end of the strap in her mouth. Tugging, losing it, tugging again, she was finally able to pull it back far enough to unfasten the buckle. The watch fell away. She wiggled one hand out of the tie. With that hand she ripped away the knotted tail-rope from her other wrist. Then quickly she freed her bound ankles.

Cassie jumped up without thinking. Immediately, she ducked back to the floor, coughing and blinking her eyes. The smoke was thick and deadly. Only on the floor was there enough air to survive.

The room was pitch dark. Heat from the crackling flames began to lick around her. Her face felt sunburned and her whole body dripped with perspiration from the heat and her fear.

If there was only something that she could use to

cover her face. She began to crawl. Her hand came to rest on a roll of . . . fur? It didn't matter. Whatever it was had escaped the flames so far, or perhaps it wasn't flammable.

Glancing around frantically for any clue as to where the door was located, she strained her eyes for light. Any light. If she continued to crawl without knowing where she was going, she would waste precious time. And she could crawl right into the worst of the inferno.

A dim line of yellow light was like a life line, reaching out to her, beckoning. It had to be light from the hallway. Outside. I must get outside! she thought. Hope flickered.

She wrapped her whole body with the blanket of fur, and started to roll toward the thin yellow line.

Whump! She slammed against a wall. Reaching out of the fur, she felt for a doorjamb. Then she pressed her palm against the door. It wasn't hot, which meant that the fire was confined to the wardrobe room. It wasn't raging in the hall, too. With the blanket still over her head, she rose to her knees, felt around until she found the doorknob, then flung the door open and tumbled out.

Gratefully she tossed off the blanket and took several deep breaths of air. Standing, she ran for the building exit.

"Help, help me!" she cried, stumbling, squinting because of the bright sunlight.

"Get some oxygen over here, on the double!" yelled a voice.

Cassie blinked and focused on Hank, the studio security guard she had talked to earlier. He jumped from a scooter, just ahead of a fire truck. Two paramedics with a tank of oxygen were close on his heels.

At that moment there was a fierce, crackling noise and a loud boom. Everyone turned to look.

"Wow, Miss Best, if you were in there, you got out just in time."

Cassie watched, horrified, as the building's ceiling caved in on itself. One of the paramedics handed her a plastic mask, and she took the cold, smooth material automatically.

"Here, breathe into this. You'll be fine. Your hands—you were in there, weren't you?"

Cassie looked at her sooty hands and wrists, which were red and raw from the ties. She breathed the oxygen until her lungs cleared, and the oxygen in her bloodstream reached her brain. Thoughts clicked back in, thoughts of how lucky she had been. Just a few minutes more in that building, and she'd have been . . . Her knees started to shake, and the paramedic grabbed her, thinking she was going to faint.

"You okay? Might be a good idea to have a doctor check you out, miss. What are those marks on your wrists?"

"Nothing, it's nothing. I just feel a little queasy—and grateful. Thanks." She returned the mask to him. "I'm all right though."

Cassie watched as the fire fighters directed a powerful stream of water into the blazing inferno.

"Why did you go inside, anyway?" Hank asked. "That old warehouse hasn't been used since the days of *Space Squadron* and *Jungle Mission*. And now all of a sudden it's a real popular place."

Cassie's mind was clearing fast. "Hank, did you see anyone here earlier?"

"I saw Rod Taggart and Tanya Grant coming from this direction about half an hour ago," answered Hank. "And someone else followed them about ten minutes later."

Cassandra waited impatiently for Hank to identify the third person. "Was it someone you recognized?"

Hank laughed. "Miss Best, it wasn't a person at all."

"What do you mean?"

"Well, technically, it was a person, but it was wearing a gorilla costume." He laughed again, apparently thinking nothing of seeing lions, tigers, and bears wandering around the lot.

"So you saw a gorilla," Cassie said.

"Yeah, one of those real-life type costumes. Real pity about that wardrobe building. Some of those costumes can never be replaced. And I'll bet the only gorilla suit that escaped the fire is the one I saw hobbling off not too long ago.''

''A gorilla,'' said Cassie, ''hobbling. You mean limping?''

Hank nodded. ''You've got it, Miss Best. A lame gorilla. He was limping, all right.''

Twice, Cassie thought. The same person has now tried to kill me twice.

***W**hen* she returned to
the *Witches' Brew* set, Cassie expected to find the
lights on and the cameras rolling. After all, the fire
had been far enough away for the other buildings to
have escaped danger, and Tanya Grant's remark that
"the show must go on" was true. Maybe they'd
stopped shooting long enough to find out what was
in flames, but then everyone had probably heard the
sirens and seen the fire truck. Once they knew that
everything was under control, they would have nat-
urally returned to work.

Cassie was mistaken. Actors and extras were sitting on the sidelines or milling around. They were
all in costume and makeup, but the set was dark.
Crew members were standing around joking and
drinking soda. But no one was filming, and Marty
Ingram was nowhere to be seen.

Alex was seated on a canvas chair off in a corner
and scribbling as she worked on her story. She
jumped when Cassie arrived. "I didn't see you! I

was so busy with my story—'' She stopped and gasped. ''Cassandra! What happened to you?''

''Oh, I . . . I . . .'' Cassie sank into the empty chair alongside Alex and said, ''A gorilla with a limp tried to finish the job he or she started in Marty's Jacuzzi. And this time it almost worked.'' She told Alex every detail, from her overhearing Rod and Tanya in the deserted costume building, to her confrontation with the gorilla and her escape from the fire.

''Cassandra!'' Alex's expression was one of shock and sympathy for her friend. ''I heard sirens, but I had no idea you were in danger!'' She squeezed Cassie's wrist. ''Oh, Cassandra, you're certain you're all right?''

''I'm fine. I just wish I knew why a limping gorilla is after me!'' Cassie headed for a bathroom to clean up as best she could. Alex followed, still talking.

''Look,'' said Alex, ''you know the saying about cats having nine lives? Well, let's pretend you're a cat. In which case you've used up two of yours since you got here. So from now on, we're in this together. We'll go everywhere in twos, as if we're twins.''

''Or stunt-doubles?'' asked Cassie. ''That could be dangerous too, Alex.'' It made her think of Sky Bowman. ''Any word from the hospital?''

''The hospital rang up a short while ago. It looks as though Sky will pull through after all. That's why we're on a break now. Marty wanted to ring Sky's room and talk with him personally. Send his regards, the company's good wishes, that sort of thing."

After Cassie had washed up and collected herself in the cast lounge, the girls walked back onto the set and right into the middle of a raging storm. The crew was set up for another, smaller coven scene, when Rod would start spying on the evildoers. The cave set was the same, and the dozen or so extras all wore the same hoods as before.

Marty Ingram was pacing around, kicking over chairs, and yelling, "Well, where is he, then? Five minutes ago, he's on the set and working. Next thing I know, he's gone! Disappeared! What in the world is going on?"

All around, the cast and crew stood silently. The lights were on, and everything was ready for the shooting of the scene. Everything but the star.

"Rod better have a good excuse when he finally does show up!" Marty raved on, putting his foot through one of the Styrofoam rocks. "Somebody fix that!" he yelled, as he pulled his foot back out.

Cassie and Alex made their way over to Tanya, who looked totally unnerved. "What happened?" asked Alex.

"Rod's just disappeared!" she said to the girls as they approached. "He's vanished into thin air. I don't know what to do! Rod's gone, and Marty's furious at me, and . . ." Tanya dissolved into tears.

"Did anyone see him leave?" Cassie asked. "Marty said he disappeared between takes."

"Nobody," Tanya said. "This isn't like Rod," she said in a choking voice. "I'm afraid something's happened to him!"

"We'll find him, don't you worry," Cassie promised, putting a hand on Tanya's shoulder. "Come on, Alex."

The two girls threaded their way through the crowd as Marty continued to rant. "I may as well move on to a new picture," he shouted. *"Witches' Brew* has been jinxed from the start, and this is just the last straw!"

"Let's check Rod's dressing room first," said Cassie as they left the set and walked down the hallway. "Maybe we'll find something to tell us why Rod left so suddenly. Or where he might have gone." Cassie kept her voice light, but she shared Tanya's fear that Rod might be in real danger. Could he have met with a final "accident"?

The girls found nothing out of the ordinary in Rod's dressing room. So they checked the other dressing rooms along the hall, the cast lounge, and the executive offices. They even had one of the janitors check all the bathrooms. No luck.

Perplexed, they returned to the set. Marty was looking at his watch and tapping his foot. Everybody in the huge soundstage was quiet. When Cassie and Alex came in, three dozen heads turned to look at them.

"Do *you* know where Rod Taggart is?" Marty said sarcastically.

"Er, no," Alex stammered.

Marty looked at his watch. "All right, that's it!" he screamed. "It's a wrap for today. I'm not going to pay a hundred people to stand around and wait for Mr. Superstar to show up. All of you, get out of here! Now!"

As the cast and crew shuffled off toward the exit doors, Marty came striding over to Tanya, who sat with her head in her hands. "If our 'star' decides to show his face again today, I'll be in my office, understand?"

Tanya nodded miserably, not even looking up. With a snort, Marty made for the exit, slamming the door behind him.

"Did you check to see if he left the studio lot?" Cassie asked Tanya.

"Yes, and he's still on the grounds," Tanya said, getting up to go. "But I can't imagine what might have happened to him. Or maybe I *can* imagine," she added grimly.

As Cassie watched Tanya walk away, she felt there must be something else she could do to find Rod.

"Alex, I've got a hunch," she said suddenly. "We

must have overlooked a clue in Rod's dressing room.''

''But we were just there,'' said Alex, surprised.

''I feel certain we missed something, Alex. Want to go back with me?''

''Definitely!''

But as Cassie and Alex ran down the hallway, they nearly bumped right into Holly Chiswick on her way out of her dressing room.

''Oh!'' Holly gave a little scream and staggered backward.

Cassie and Alex rushed to grab her before she fell. ''Are you all right?'' Cassie asked, helping Holly to her feet.

''I'm fine,'' Holly breathed. ''You just startled me, that's all. First Sky is shot, and then Rod disappears. It's all making me very nervous. . . .'' Her voice trailed off uncertainly. ''Well, if you'll excuse me . . .'' She started off down the hall.

Cassie noticed that Holly *wasn't limping!* ''Holly!'' she called out. ''How's your foot this afternoon?''

''My foot?'' repeated Holly, perplexed. Then she said, ''Oh! I know what you mean. But the question should be how's my *boot.*''

Cassie glanced down at Holly's feet. ''But you're not wearing boots now.''

''And that's why I'm not limping,'' Holly said. ''I ought to know better than to break in a new pair of boots when I'm working on a picture, but I didn't, and this morning my feet were killing me!"

"Oh," said Cassie. She wondered if Holly was telling the truth. It certainly sounded like a plausible explanation.

"Well, then. Bye! I think I'll go look for Rod." Holly hurried off.

Funny, thought Cassie. Everybody's looking for Rod. I wonder who's going to find him. . . .

It took the girls only another minute to reach Rod's dressing room. It was still empty, but this time, Cassie noticed some things she'd missed before, when they'd been in such a rush.

For instance, she saw that Rod's jacket, the one he wore in the scene, was draped over the chair in front of the makeup table. "He came back here first," Cassie told Alex, feeling in the jacket pockets for any clues. The pockets were empty.

"Look at this!" Alex said, pointing to a pencil on the makeup table.

"That's it!" Cassie said. "That's what I overlooked! I'll bet Rod wrote a message!" She gave the area a quick search. "But if he did, how come it isn't here? Wouldn't it be on the table, or stuck to the mirror?"

"Yes," Alex said. "Unless somebody else got the message before we did. . . ."

"Or," Cassie added, "unless he left it somewhere else—like the bulletin board!"

"Right!" Alex cried.

In milliseconds, the girls were out in the hall, examining the message board. Sure enough, there, for anyone who was looking to see, was a scrap of notepaper. On it was scrawled a message:

> *If you want me,*
> *Try Soundstage C*
> *At five past three.*

"Alex!" cried Cassie triumphantly. "It must be from Rod!"

"Hold on, Cassandra," said Alex. "It could be from anyone. And it could have been here for days."

"Did you see it before?"

"No."

"Neither did I," Cassie said. "Don't you think one of us would have noticed it?"

"I suppose you're right," Alex said, "but what if it's not from Rod? What if it's from the person behind the other notes?"

"Those notes were typed, remember?" Cassie pointed out. "This one's handwritten—in pencil. And it's not addressed to Rod, the way the others were. It has no name on it at all."

The two girls stood there, looking at each other, then at the note. Cassie took it off the wall. "This may come in handy as evidence," she said, pocketing it.

Then she looked at her watch. "Ten to three. We've got fifteen minutes. . . ."

Alex looked alarmed. "Cassie!" she said. "What are you going to do? With all that's happened around here, I'm scared, really scared. Please don't take any risks!"

Cassie frowned. "All right, Alex. I'll alert studio security, you call the police. Tell them to be at Soundstage C at, oh, say, ten after three. That'll give us five minutes to listen in on whatever's going on."

Alex looked frightened. "I hope you know what you're doing, Cassandra. Where shall we meet?"

"Back here, in ten minutes."

"Right. Cassandra—"

"Don't worry, Alex. This is our big break."

*W*hile Alex went to Rod's dressing room to call the police, Cassie went hunting for someone from studio security. The guard who should have been on duty in front of the building was nowhere to be seen.

"Just my luck," Cassie muttered under her breath. "Never one around when you need them."

She went to a phone booth and tried the Majestic Pictures switchboard, but they put her on hold for what seemed like hours, until finally Cassie just gave up, slamming down the phone in frustration.

Just then she heard a familiar voice behind her. "Whoa, there, Miss Best. What seems to be the trouble?"

Hank!

"Oh, Hank, you don't know how glad I am to see you!" she gasped, hugging the surprised security guard. "I don't have time to explain, but please, can you get a security man down to Soundstage C at exactly ten after three? Better make that an armed security man.''

''Call out the heavy artillery, huh?''

''That's right.''

''But I don't understand—''

''I told you, Hank, I can't explain right now. But please—it's urgent. Trust me.''

The earnestness in Cassie's voice was convincing. ''Well, all right,'' Hank agreed. ''I'll call in the request. I hope you know what you're doing, though.''

''Believe me, Hank, I do.''

''Oh, by the way,'' said the security guard. ''A call came in for you, from London. The guy said it was urgent.''

Urgent! ''Thanks,'' she said, going back into the phone booth and dialing the number on the message slip Hank had handed her. Alex was waiting for her, but what Peter had to tell her might be vital to the case. Besides, she still had three minutes to spare.

''Peter, it's Cassandra!'' she said when she heard his voice on the other end of the line. This time, the connection was terrible. She could barely hear his voice through the static, but there was no time to call him back.

''Cassandra, I have news,'' he said excitedly. ''I've been digging around for information about the insurance for that film of yours, and guess what I found. Mxiapanalesf . . ."

"Peter!" Cassie called into the phone. "Could you please repeat that? I couldn't quite hear you!"

Cassie glanced at her watch again. One minute to go!

"I said, the pouistrflacofumpy had an insurance policy for *triple* the amount in the event of the picture closing down."

"Who?" Cassie cried. "Who had the policy? Peter, say it real loudly, would you?"

"I said, the production company!" came the distant voice.

Cassie stood there, frozen. *The production company!*

"Cassandra, are you there?"

"Thanks, Peter!" Cassie shouted into the phone. "Thanks a billion jillion! You've just helped me solve the case!" Before he could respond, Cassie had hung up the phone and was tearing across the lot to meet Alex.

Now Cassie knew everything. For the first time, all the bizarre events of the past few days made perfect, crystal-clear sense.

And for the first time, Cassie could see that someone besides Rod Taggart had a reason for wanting the movie to fold. An even bigger reason than Rod's.

Cassie also knew something else. She knew that,

at that very moment, Rod Taggart was in mortal danger.

"Where in the world have you been?" cried Alex as Cassie arrived at the message board. "Do you realize what time it is? We've probably missed everything!"

"Never mind, let's run!" Cassie said, leading the way outside and across the road to Soundstage C.

"What time have you got?" Alex called as they went.

"I've got ten after three," said Cassie. "How about you?"

"Mine says seven after, and it's super-accurate," Alex replied.

Either way, they were late.

"I know who's behind everything!" Cassie called back over her shoulder. "I spoke to Peter, and he told me the production company's got an even bigger policy than Rod has against the picture's not being completed."

"No kidding!" said Alex, as they reached the building and went inside, headed for the inner door of the soundstage itself. "So tell me—who *is* behind it all?"

"You'll see," said Cassie, her hand on the doorknob. "Are you ready, Alex?"

Alex gave Cassie a quick smile. "Ready as I'll ever be, Cassandra Best."

Cassie pushed open the door, and the two of them went inside.

Rod Taggart was standing center stage. Directly opposite, holding him at gunpoint, was someone wearing a long robe, one of the extras' costumes from *Witches' Brew.* Angry eyes glared out from behind a lifelike gorilla mask. Cassie had seen that mask before.

*T*he "gorilla" whirled around and was caught off guard. But both of its hands lifted the gun to shoot. Quickly Rod brought up his left fist and knocked the weapon into the air. His captor lunged at Rod, and the two went to the floor.

"Right ankle!" yelled Cassie. "Kick it, Rod!"

Rod obeyed. The "gorilla" let out a loud moan. And as its hands went reflexively to its ankle, Rod wrestled his prisoner into a hammerlock.

Cassie saw where the gun had landed and rushed forward to grab it. "Hands up!" she cried, half surprised at her own bravery. "I mean it! Over your head, or I'll shoot!" She hoped the threat sounded convincing; she'd never fired a gun before in her life and didn't want to start now.

The gorilla reluctantly raised its hands in the air. At that moment the door to Soundstage C opened and an armed security guard and Marty Ingram came rushing in.

"I've got him now," said the guard, grabbing the "gorilla."

Cassie set down the gun among a few other prop pistols lying on a table. Then, sinking into a chair, she exclaimed, "I've never been so glad to see anyone!"

Rod stood up and brushed himself off. "It's a good thing I've been doing my own stunts!"

The security guard moved forward and reached for the gorilla mask.

"Be careful!" warned Marty. "Whoever this is may be carrying another weapon."

There was angry mumbling but the lifelike mask muffled both the words and voice. While the guard held his prisoner, Rod gave a tug at the back of the mask and yanked it off.

"*Jeff Ryan!*" cried Marty, Alex, and Rod all at once.

Cassie wasn't shocked. Instead, she nodded. "The bigger they are, the harder they fall. You couldn't resist, could you, Jeff?"

"What are you talking about?" he snarled.

"Your puns. I didn't figure it out with the first note because I knew someone could have used the pun to make you look guilty when you weren't. But you couldn't resist the temptation to pun again. And when I found out about your insurance—"

"Insurance? What insurance?" Marty wanted to know.

"As head of the production company, Jeff took out an insurance policy that would have paid him triple if the film folded," Cassie said. "Of course, Rod has the same type of insurance. . . ."

"Just a sec," said Rod. "The only reason I took out an insurance policy is because Tanya begged me to. There have been lots of accidents on film sets over the past years, especially on action movies with dangerous stunts." Then he shook his head and asked, "You mean you suspected *me*?"

Alex said, "Well, we didn't know what to think."

Suddenly Jeff piped up. "It *was* him!" he said. "He lured me here and held me up with the gun. I managed to get it away from him, and then you two girls walked in—"

"Wrong, Jeff," Cassie corrected him. "You were the one in the wardrobe room wearing a gorilla suit. And you tried to shoot us when we came in, remember?"

"No!" cried Jeff. "I was just startled! And this is the first time I put on this costume, I swear. I . . . I . . ." He faltered, sensing that nobody was buying his farfetched story.

"You caused those accidents on the set, Jeff," Cassie insisted. "You tried to close down the picture by scaring off the star. And when he got angry instead, and insisted on continuing with the picture, you tried to get rid of him for real."

Jeff snorted. "You don't have a shred of evidence against me, kid," he said.

"If the bullet taken from Sky Bowman's body matches the bullets in your gun, that ought to be enough to convict you of attempted murder," said Cassie.

"Ha!" Jeff laughed. "Wrong again, Miss Know-It-All. Anyone could have taken that gun and used it without me finding out. I keep it in an unlocked drawer in my office. No jury in the world would convict me on that alone!"

Just then, two policemen came in, their guns drawn. "There's your man," said Cassie. "I suspect he's the one who shot Sky Bowman."

The police went over and put handcuffs on Jeff. "You've got the wrong man!" Jeff protested, as they helped him out of his long robe and frisked him.

"Maybe so," said one of the policemen. "You can tell us your story down at the station house. Hey, hurt your ankle recently?"

Cassie nodded. There, on Jeff's ankle, was a huge Ace bandage.

"Just a sprain," grumbled the producer. "That doesn't prove anything!" he called out to Cassie.

"Maybe not," Cassie put in, "but whoever tried to drown me in Marty's Jacuzzi walked with a limp. So did the robed figure who shot Sky Bowman. And so did the 'gorilla' who tied me up and set fire to the costume building. That's too much limping, and too much gorilla, to be a coincidence. It should also be more than enough proof to put you in prison for a good long time.''

Cassie thought back to Marty's pool party. Jeff had left ahead of Alex and her. Did he leave early so they wouldn't see him limping? And was his hurt foot the reason why he had stayed seated on the set the next day?

Now Cassie realized that she hadn't seen Jeff Ryan standing on two feet or walking since Marty's party!

''What happened, Jeff?'' she asked. ''Did you sprain your ankle at Marty's house when you and Rod had your fight? And what was the fight about, anyway?''

Jeff Ryan sputtered, but he didn't answer. Instead, Rod said, ''Our fight was really dumb, Cassandra. Jeff accused me of staging my own accidents to get publicity for myself. I was so angry with him, well, I punched him. I didn't know I'd wind up in the pool. I just lost my temper, and—''

''And you kicked him in the ankle, didn't you?'' said Alex.

''I guess so. But I didn't realize it was enough to cause a limp,'' answered Rod.

Cassie noticed that throughout her speech and afterward, too, while Rod was talking, Jeff kept glaring at Marty Ingram. Marty pointedly ignored him.

''You know, Jeff,'' Cassie said, ''what I can't figure out is why you tried to kill me. Did you think I knew too much?'' Before Jeff could answer, she hurried on. ''When the Jacuzzi didn't work, you tried fire. That gorilla mask is identical to the one I saw just before you put me under—what was it, chloroform? Oh, well, it hardly matters. What I don't understand is why? How did you know I was stalking you so early on in the game?'' Cassie paused, hoping that by playing dumb she would encourage Jeff to talk. Her ploy worked.

Jeff glanced over at Marty Ingram again. ''Tell her, partner,'' he growled.

''*Partner!*'' Marty gasped. ''What in the world are you talking about?''

''Forget it, Marty!'' yelled Jeff. ''I'm not taking this rap all by myself! You came up with the bright idea to shut down the picture. We'd both be better off, you said.''

''You're out of your mind, Jeff,'' said Marty quietly, laughing it off. ''I've been working on plans for this movie all year! Why would I want to shut it down?''

Cassie looked directly at him and said, ''For the insurance money that you would have received as a partner in the production company. It would have been very helpful in paying off those gambling debts.'' Cassie remembered Holly's story about Marty at the blackjack table.

''What gambling debts? You're writing a fantasy

script, Cass!" Marty laughed, but he sounded nervous.

"The debts you were discussing on the phone during the party at your house," said Cassie.

"When you were stupid enough to let her eavesdrop outside your study!" Jeff shouted angrily. "I told you I saw her in the mirror!"

It all makes sense! thought Cassie. Jeff and Marty didn't know that I didn't hear or see enough to understand what Marty was talking about. Or to whom. They were afraid to take the chance, so Jeff put on a robe and tried to drown me!

"The waiter at the party gave me a perfect clue," said Cassie.

"What was that?" asked Alex, scribbling notes on her scratchpad.

"The waiter was an actor, and he told me that Marty redecorates as soon as one of his movies wraps. Well, *Witches' Brew* only started shooting a couple of weeks ago, but he's already refurnished with a Spanish motif. In the style of his *next* film."

"Go on," said Marty. "I'm enjoying this."

"Give it up, Marty," Jeff called out. "The bigger they are, the harder they fall—and if I've got to fall, you're going to fall with me, pal."

"Oh, is that so?" Marty said with a smile. But his quivering lip gave away his growing desperation.

"It sure is," Jeff shot back. "It just so happens I took the precaution of taping some of our most interesting conversations. I figured, better safe than sorry. Right, pal?''

''Why, you little—'' With a quick move, Marty ran over to the prop table and grabbed a gun, pointing it straight at Cassie. ''All right, nobody move!'' he ordered. ''Or the little amateur detective gets it!''

He looked over at the security guard and the policemen. ''Drop your weapons, gentlemen,'' he said calmly. ''You wouldn't want this young lady's life on your hands, would you?''

Obediently, the police and the guard dropped their guns to the floor.

''That's right, guys.'' Marty nodded. Then he glanced over at Jeff Ryan. Marty's face was white with rage. ''I should never have brought you into this, you punning moron. You've spoiled everything with your bull-headed violence!''

Jeff said nothing. He was as scared as everyone else in the room. Obviously, Marty Ingram meant business.

''Now,'' Marty said, ''up against the wall. Everybody move together—slowly. No tricks.''

Cassie glanced at the gun in Marty's hand. Do I dare? she wondered. If one of us doesn't act now, it'll be too late, because Marty is about to make his exit. This is your last chance, Cassandra Best. Here goes.

''You know, Marty,'' she began, ''you're not a bad director.'' She purposely moved a step or two closer to him. "But there's one thing even a good director can overlook."

"Quit stalling, Cass," said Marty, "and stay with the others." He was gesturing toward the wall where Rod, Alex, and the others stood. Jeff Ryan was off to one side, but he was handcuffed, so Cassie wasn't worried about him.

Come on, Marty! urged Cassie mentally. Take the bait! A good director is always curious.

"Okay, Cass," said Marty, "you've got me. What did I overlook?"

"Your props, Marty," she answered. "You forgot to check your props. And, to borrow a pun from Jeff, you've drawn a blank."

"I've what?"

"You've drawn a blank. That's a prop gun you're holding. It isn't loaded."

"Cute," said Marty. "I've used that in a dozen films. But nobody falls for it anymore."

"Marty, the real gun is still on the table where I put it when you and the guard arrived." Cassie spoke her lines so matter-of-factly that she almost convinced herself.

"Where'd you get the plot for this?" asked Marty.

From the story of *Ali Baba and the Forty Thieves*, Cassie was thinking. And all the jars marked with an X. But she didn't say a word aloud.

Whether she'd convinced Marty, she couldn't tell.

Apparently, though, she'd convinced the others; Cassie could see from the expressions in their eyes.

She shot a quick glance toward the policeman in charge. If Marty opened the chamber and found bullets inside, her bluff would be over. But if the policeman acted quickly enough—in the split second it would take for Marty to examine the gun or check out the prop table—they'd all have a chance.

It was so quiet on the soundstage that Cassie could hear her own heartbeat drumming inside her ears.

Nobody moved a muscle. Even Jeff Ryan seemed to have turned to stone.

Marty was locked into a staring match with Cassie. But she could see the twitching of his right eyelid.

That means he's nervous, she thought, staring back.

And nervous means he's not sure.

"You're smart, Cass," admitted Marty, still not removing his eyes from her, nor his finger from the trigger.

Cassie didn't answer; she just continued to stare him down.

"There's just one thing," he said at last to the officers without turning his gaze toward them. "If the gun isn't loaded, why hasn't one of you guys jumped me?"

"Because like you," Cassie replied with the utmost calm, "they can't be certain it's the wrong gun. I'm the only one who knows." Come on! she thought. I can't keep up this act forever!

Finally, more from instinct than from anything Marty did, Cassie sensed that he was about to falter. For a fraction of a second, his eyelids fluttered, as though he were deciding whether to check the other guns on the table or to take a chance with the one in his hand.

Cassie was afraid the gambler in him would win out.

Very slowly, she inched toward the fire extinguisher hanging on the wall just behind her.

In the blinking of an eye—Marty's eye—Cassie grabbed the red cannister and took aim.

*C*assie turned the nozzle and sprayed the white chemical foam for all it was worth. All over Marty.

Rod pounced on the director and they both grappled for the gun.

It fell to the floor with a thud, and Cassie kicked it out of reach. She took aim and sprayed again.

Marty Ingram, looking like Frosty the Snowman, punched Rod, who landed a fist in the director's eye. Marty lurched forward and barreled into Rod's stomach. Both men tumbled into a heap. Now they were rolling in a sea of ammonium phosphate "whitecaps."

By now, though, the policemen and security guard had found their own guns beneath the chemical suds, and the officer in charge yelled, "Freeze!"

A handcuffed Jeff Ryan was almost at the door, but the order stopped him cold.

"Okay, everybody!" called Rod. "It's a wrap!"

As the police led Jeff Ryan and Marty Ingram to

a squad car waiting outside, Rod and the girls headed across the lot to Soundstage A. They found Tanya Grant pacing back and forth in Rod's dressing room.

"Oh! You're safe!" she cried, running to Rod. "What happened? You look terrible!"

Rod gave a short laugh. "If you think *I* look terrible, you ought to see Marty!"

He went into the bathroom and washed his hands and face, then flopped down onto the sofa, where Tanya joined him.

"I want to hear the whole story," Tanya said. "Everything, from start to finish."

After Rod had explained, Cassie said, "Now that you're telling the whole story, tell me what you and Tanya were arguing about in the old wardrobe building before Jeff set it on fire," said Cassie. "What were you two doing in that deserted building, anyway?"

"Looking for a bit of privacy to talk," said Tanya. "That's hard to find with Rod, these days."

"Tanya was trying to talk me out of handling things myself," Rod explained. "She begged me to walk off the picture and let the police handle it."

"But he's stubborn," Tanya broke in. "And as macho as they come. He kept on insisting he could handle it himself."

"How would it have looked to my fans, Tanya?" Rod protested. "Me walking off a picture, then col-

143

lecting double my money from the insurance company? My fans look at me as a hero, as I think I told you, Cassandra. I couldn't have them see me as a victim, much less a greedy victim!''

Everyone laughed at the image of Rod Taggart skulking away from the Majestic lot with his moneybags under his arm. Even Cassie had to admit to herself that Rod had a point.

"Still," she insisted, "you wouldn't have been much good to your fans as a corpse."

"You're dead right there," Rod said. "Oops—that old Jeff Ryan punning magic . . .''

"You know, Rod," Tanya said, "maybe your next film should be a comedy."

"Amen to that!" Rod agreed.

"By the way, Rod, did the hotel doctor ever report back to you on the contents of the sugar packet?" Cassie asked. "I'm curious."

"Yes," Rod said. "He told me it was a strong sedative, not poison. Still could have killed me, though, if I'd taken it all."

Alex had taken out her spiral notebook and pencil again. "Listen, Rod," she said, "I'm sure you don't feel up to an interview at the moment, but Daddy *is* expecting a story, and I have one blank sheet of paper left."

"Yeah. Well, go ahead, Alex," he offered. "Ask away." He squeezed Tanya's hand, and Cassie, watching Alex, wondered if her question was going to be about the production secretary and the male lead of *Witches' Brew*.

"What made you write that note?" asked Alex. "And what made you think the right person would show up?"

"Just a gamble, really," said Rod with a shrug. "I had to try something. And you must admit, it worked like a charm. Except I didn't really think it through. I should have known whoever showed up would have a gun."

"Well, you can't think of everything," Alex quipped.

"No, not even Marty and Jeff thought of everything," Rod agreed. "They covered every possible angle, but there was one thing they didn't count on."

"And what was that?" asked Tanya, gazing up into Rod's eyes.

"Miss Cassandra Best," said Rod. "The best detective in Hollywood."

"Detective?" gasped Tanya. "You mean—"

"Yes," Cassie admitted. "Alex asked me to come out here. She was afraid for Rod, and of course, we wanted as few people as possible to know."

"That's okay, I forgive you," said Tanya. "You certainly did a wonderful job."

"She's the 'best'!" Alex crowed, giving her friend a hug.

After Alex had FAXed her story to London, the

girls' next stop was the hospital, to see how Sky Bowman was getting on. Rod and Tanya stayed behind for a top-level meeting with the owners of Majestic Studios.

Alex and Cassie found Sky sitting up in bed with Holly at his side. He was feeling much better, and when the girls told him how the mystery had turned out, he said he was ready to get up and dance.

Soon, though, Sky settled down, and his face took on a serious look. "I wonder if they'll scrap the whole project," he said.

"There'll always be another movie, once you're up and about," Holly reminded him. Now that Sky was recovering and Rod had been found, she looked much more relaxed. "The doctor said you'll have to take it easy for a while, though. And in case you don't get the message, that means no stunt work."

"The doctor also said because I'm young and strong, I'll heal quickly," countered Sky. "Maybe no car-chase scenes or leaps across buildings for a few weeks, but—"

"A few weeks!" Holly blurted out. But then she saw Sky crossing his eyes to tease her, and she laughed with relief.

"Alex and I have some business to take care of," said Cassie, "so we'll leave the two of you alone for now. We're glad you're better, Sky. See you back at the studio, Holly."

When they were in the elevator, Alex said, "You know, Cassandra, I've always seen Holly as a shallow starlet. But she's really quite a sweet person."

Cassie smiled. "And so, Miss Bennett, are you."

Now that the case was solved, Cassie thought she'd be returning to Milltown. But that night, while she and Alex, dressed in two of Alex's most beautiful dresses, were finishing dinner in the elegant hotel dining room, Rod and Tanya stopped by their table.

"May we join you?" asked Rod. "Just for a minute?"

Alex and Cassie moved over in the tufted leather banquette to make room for their two guests.

"Now that Marty and Jeff are busy sending each other to jail," began Rod, "we're going to make a few changes on the set. Beginning with this."

Tanya smiled secretively as Rod handed Cassie a large envelope. Inside was a script, covered in black leatherette and titled in gold-embossed letters.

"*Witches' Brew*," she read aloud, looking questioningly from Rod to Tanya.

"Open it," said Rod.

Cassie turned to the first page. The characters' names were printed as they had been before, but some cast changes and additions had been noted with pen and ink.

Marty Ingram's name as director had been crossed out. In its place was written *Rod Taggart*.

"Congratulations, Rod!" Cassie said. "That's terrific!"

"Keep reading," said Rod mysteriously.

Rod's selection as director had come as a surprise. But the bigger surprise was a line added to the bottom of the list. On the left side of the page was the name of a new character. Opposite, on the right side, read the name *Cassandra Best*!

"Rod!" said Cassie. "What a sweet thought!"

"Sweet has nothing to do with it," Rod continued. "After the way you handled yourself with Marty and the pistol bluff, I feel certain you could act as well on film."

"*Whaaat*? You mean . . . you mean this *isn't* just a souvenir?" Her voice had gone up at least an octave.

Rod was laughing now. "Don't get *that* excited, Cassandra—Holly is still playing the lead! But the way you just spoke is exactly the way I want you to say your lines on camera! It's perfect!"

On camera!

Rod was going to direct, and he'd given Cassie a speaking role in the film!

The following day Alex slept late. Cassie had to be at the studio before dawn. She was sent first to

148

the wardrobe room, where this time she was outfitted in white satin.

From wardrobe Cassie went to the makeup room, from there to the hairdresser, and finally to the set.

Cassie had one long scene between her and Holly, where Holly would lure her from the coven back to the real world. To prepare, Cassie kept saying her lines over and over as the morning wore on: ''But I'm so afraid!'' she whispered as the hairdresser styled her hair. ''They'll kill me if they find out I've left them!'' She must have repeated her lines a hundred times, but neither the hairdresser nor the makeup lady said anything to her. They were used to actors talking out loud.

When Cassie got to the set, Rod had her rehearse the scene with Holly. ''Break a leg,'' whispered Holly as the two of them took their positions.

They were ready to shoot.

Rod took his place beside the cameraman, and called, ''Roll film, scene forty-two.''

The clapper stepped in front of the actors and said, ''*Witches' Brew*, scene forty-two, take one.'' Then he clapped the chalkboard and stepped out of range as the camera began to roll.

''Action!'' came Rod's voice from the darkness.

Cassie felt a surge of electricity pass through her body as she spoke the lines she'd been rehearsing all morning. She barely knew what she was saying, or even where she was—it all seemed so unreal to her, and yet so incredibly real, all at the same time!

"Cut!" Rod yelled when Cassie and Holly were finished. "Great! Print it!"

Cassie couldn't believe it had all happened so fast. Her speaking debut in movies, and they'd gotten it in a single take!

Chapter
15

*T*he hardest part was saying good-bye. Cassie had been in Hollywood for less than a week and so much had happened.

She'd solved the mystery, and that was exciting.

But most of all, she'd made new friends and discovered a whole new world.

Tanya arranged for a small party on the set of *Witches' Brew*, and as "Cassandra Best" shook hands with the many members of the crew, she was reminded of how much work actually went into the making of a movie.

Then came the moment to say farewell. There were hugs and handshakes all around. Tanya and Rod were last.

"Thanks for all your help," said Tanya. She handed Cassandra a small manila envelope. "Here's that special item you asked for." She winked, and then nudged Rod.

On cue, he said, "And we thought you'd like this for yourself. A real Hollywood souvenir."

151

Cassie ripped open the package Rod gave her and found a red *Witches' Brew* T-shirt inside.

"We have one for you, too, Alex," Rod continued. "Tanya and I are grateful to you as well, for bringing Cassandra onto the case."

Later, when she and Alex reached the Los Angeles International Airport, it took all the acting talent Cassie could muster to keep her tears from showing. She hid them behind her sunglasses, the ones she'd bought on her trip to England.

"With those glasses, Cassandra," teased Alex, "you really look the part."

"What part is that?" asked Cassie.

"A star!" said Alex dramatically, making Cassie burst into laughter.

Saying good-bye to Alex in Los Angeles was even more difficult than it had been in London or Lexington, Kentucky. But now it was because of their closeness, not because Cassie wondered whether she'd ever see Alexandra again or if she'd ever have another mystery to solve. She knew it was only a matter of time before she'd do both.

As soon as she boarded the plane, Cassie settled back in her first-class seat and closed her eyes. After lunch was served, she decided to nap. Before she knew it, she was awakened by the captain's announcement: "Please fasten your seat belts. We are approaching Milltown Airport."

Cassie yawned, then she peered out the window on her right.

Wait a minute! she thought. Am I dreaming? She blinked and looked out again.

Sure enough, as the plane taxied up to the gate, she saw a group of around fifty teenagers. They were waving wildly in the direction of the plane. Cassie craned her neck to see what they were waving at.

Cameras! Huge klieg lights! And all kinds of cables and wires and filming equipment! They were set up and ready to shoot!

Cassie swallowed hard as Alex's words flashed through her mind.

"You'll have quite a homecoming, Cassandra," she'd said. "Especially when they learn that you've just made a film!"

"But how will anyone know?" Cassie had asked.

And Alex had replied, "Never underestimate the powers of the press."

Could the Bennett newspapers be responsible for this? she wondered.

As the possibility sank in, Cassie's stomach grew jittery.

What'll I do? My hair must be a mess after this long flight. I can't be photographed looking like this!

She took out her makeup kit and reapplied her powder and lipstick.

Now the aircraft came to a full stop, the FASTEN

SEAT BELT sign went off, and the passengers began to deplane.

Cassie's single suitcase was under her seat. She pulled it out, straightened the creases in her linen skirt, and moved toward the exit door.

"Have a nice stay," said the flight attendant.

"Thank you," answered Cassie, taking a final deep breath before facing her waiting "public."

The lights flashed on, a camera was rolling, and Cassie heard "Action!" just as she reached the exit.

What should I do? she wondered. Automatically, the actress in her sent her arm up into the air, and she waved graciously and theatrically to all those assembled below.

"Cut!" she heard a man's voice shout. "Joe, we can't see the lettering. Move the tube closer!"

Someone yelled back, "Okay, but you'll have to bring the kids in tighter!"

"Don't worry about the extras! We're getting paid to shoot the product!"

The product? thought Cassie.

Then, as she descended the steps and the person named Joe moved the "tube" into view, it all became clear. The mob of teenagers, the lights, the cameras—none of it was for Cassandra Best.

Not even for Cassie B. Jones.

A gigantic tube of toothpaste had been made to look like a small airplane. A propeller had been attached to its cap, and wings jutted out of its sides.

All this equipment—and all these people—are here to shoot *a television commercial*!

In spite of herself, Cassie burst out laughing. She couldn't stop until she was inside the arrival area and saw her father and her sister waving.

She waved back, delighted to greet her "public," and very happy to be home.

"Gran's made lemon meringue pie for dessert to-night," Melanie was saying as Martin Jones pulled into the driveway alongside the house.

"Cassie may not be interested, Mel," teased their father. "After all, now that she's made a movie, she may prefer caviar and pheasant under glass."

"Lemon meringue sounds great, Dad," said Cassie, opening her door. "You know, movie people aren't really so different from other people. And they work very hard."

"Sure they do," said Mel, climbing out of the backseat. "My heart bleeds for you!" She clutched her chest and said melodramatically, "Madame, allow me to carry your luggage."

Cassie couldn't believe her ears, but she had to believe her eyes when her sister grabbed the suitcase and started up the walk.

"Dad, is she feeling all right?" asked Cassie.

Martin Jones shrugged. "Something's strange, isn't it? She couldn't wait till you got home."

As soon as they were inside the house, Mel said,

"Cassie, you must be tired after all your movie acting and your trip. Why don't you go lie down? I'll carry your stuff upstairs."

Cassie felt her sister's forehead. "Has anyone taken your temperature lately?"

Martin Jones looked at his two daughters and laughed. "If you girls don't mind," he said, "I'll finish reading the paper before your mom and Gran get home." He went into the living room.

Cassie and Melanie headed up the stairs together. "Tell me something," said Cassie. "What's up? Why so thoughtful all of a sudden?"

"Because," answered Melanie in all seriousness as they entered the bedroom, "you're going to tell me every single detail about Rod Taggart, that's why!"

Cassie grinned and said, "It's a deal." She opened her suitcase. In the large pocket-compartment inside the lid was the manila envelope Tanya Grant had given her. And inside that was an eight-by-ten glossy photograph.

Cassie laid the picture across the pillow on Mel's bed. She could hardly wait to see her sister's reaction to the picture—and to the inscription, which read: *To Melanie, with love, from Rod Taggart.*

As her sister squealed with delight, Cassie lay back on her bed and gazed dreamily out the window. She wondered how soon she'd have the chance to be Cassandra Best again and to solve another mystery. As her thoughts drifted to Alexandra, who would soon be back in London, Cassie smiled to herself. She knew if Alex had anything to do with it—and certainly she would—that chance wasn't very far off.

The Cassandra Mysteries

Brittany